French Sauce

Wally Kasper

ISBN : 978-0993711909

About the Author

In 1941, Wally Kasper went straight from Leader, Saskatchewan High School to the Royal Canadian Air Force where he trained as a pilot. A year later, he was flying Lancaster bombers over Germany. He moved on to Spitfires and after the war to the University of Toronto where he studied philosophy and political science.

He was called back into the air force to teach NATO pilots and did a stint in intelligence in Europe during the Cold War. He left the air force in 1964 and went to work for CIDA setting up training programs in Canada for people round the world. He taught political science and philosophy courses at St. Patrick's, a junior college which fed universities.

He has written one book, *A night out with the boys*, on his war experiences. It had been excerpted for *Esprit de Corps* magazine. He has written many stories and poems for *Canadian Stories* magazine.

He lives in Ottawa.

CHAPTER ONE

The strange conjunction of people and places would have done credit to any of the ancient Greek dramatists. It might also make you believe in their ideas about gods manipulating ordinary mortals to fit preordained scenarios.

Unlike the altercation that projected Oedipus into the marriage with his mother, and unleashed the tragedy that followed, this strange story begins with a small act of kindness. It would have results almost impossible to believe in the lives of so many people. Let me spend a few moments setting the scene for the opening of this story.

I, James Warburton, age twenty-two, born and raised in Toronto, was in the final semester of a geology degree at the University. A half dozen of us, in that class of '62 had taken to going to a watering hole on Bloor Street for a beer after the ten thirty class on Thursday to do an analysis of the week's classes, and to exchange our newly acquired wisdom.

On this Thursday in early April, I stayed behind after class to ask a question of the professor. His explanation was longer and more complicated than I had imagined. I missed the group as they went for the usual pint; needed to kill any academic germs that might have crept in during the week. It was usually one pint and then off to Tim Horton's for a bowl of chili, and then back to hit the books. The final exams were looming large on the horizon.

When I arrived they were gone and the only other person in the bar room was a rather ragged, shabby looking elderly fellow sitting at a corner table. I took my pint at the bar and was about to sit down when I thought I might be sociable so I went over and said, "Mind if I join you?"

"Please do.'

Then I noticed that there was no glass or plate in front of him. Down on his luck, no doubt, I thought.

"Can I get you a beer?"

"Oh yes, please."

I did and as I sat down I stuck out my hand and said, "I'm Jim Warburton, a geology student."

"Arthur Wilkins. About twenty years ago I was where you are now–a student of geology here in Toronto." Then he saw my puzzled look, laughed and said, "I know I don't look like I've had any success as a geologist, or anything else, but it is true. After convocation I spent three years in the Army before I could get about the exploration I wanted to do on the upper reaches of the Canadian Shield."

"Sorry to interrupt, but they make a respectable roast beef sandwich here, shall I order a couple and get us another beer?"

"I would really appreciate that, but you're a student

and most students are as poor as church mice."

"My grandmother left me an inheritance months ago so I'm not hurting."

He went on "In my third summer up in northern Quebec–it was a little easier now that we could fly in and be picked up a couple months later–my partner and I came across a curious formation. On one side of a small lake fed by two small rivers, there was a rocky ridge that had been pushed almost straight up to a height of about one hundred and fifty feet. You could see the many layers from where we were in the canoe on the lake below. We tied the canoe to a big rock, and then started the difficult climb through shrubs that had taken root and up to have a closer look at the layers. I stopped to look at what seemed like a long thin layer of gold.

Bill, my partner, was a short distance ahead of me. He went around a large rock and saw a cave. He paused for a moment and turned to me and said, "There is a large layer that looks like gold or fool's gold in here," and as he spoke we heard the roar of a bear. A mother bear shot out of the cave and attacked Bill.

I grabbed my pistol, and got two shots into the bear before she knew I was there. She fell to the ground beside Bill. I pulled Bill over behind the rock where I could see him as well as any other bear that might come out. But it was too late to do anything as the bear's claws had nearly separated Bill's head from his body. After a few minutes, I wrapped Bill in his parka as best I could, and started the agonizing task of getting him back to the canoe.

It was mid afternoon by the time I was back at the other side of the lake and able to set up the radio aerial and send a MAYDAY for help. I wrapped Bill's remains in a tarp and put them high in a tree for safety, made a big fire, and then slept in the canoe.

The rescue twin Otter arrived mid morning and we made our way back to Quebec City, and then back to Toronto to report to the company. They had a surprise for me, their resident geologist in Indonesia had suffered a heart attack, and they needed a replacement. Would I go? Two days later, I had a two year contract and was on my way to an exotic new land on the other side of the world."

We had finished our sandwiches, dessert, and coffee seemed welcome so after it arrived he continued, "Two years turned into twelve and the government seemed to be very pleased with the development of their resources–especially on the larger islands of Sulawesi and Kalamantin.

The government had been generous with salary increases over the years, and I was thinking of going back home to stay when I received two bombshells.

First, I was told I had contracted a nasty case of tuberculosis and needed to get back to Canada fast and start a treatment program. I was contagious and would have to go into a secluded environment for some time.

The second bombshell arrived a month later when a new dictatorship took over the government and no foreign exchange was allowed out of the country. I was in effect a rich man who could not get his hands on a penny of his money.

I have been out of the sanatorium for six months and getting a job seems to be hopeless. You have been the first person who has been generous with your time and money."

I had been thinking, while he had been talking, about what one of the supervisors at the Royal Ontario Museum had told me months earlier about their problems in hiring good stockmen with knowledge of basic geology.

I said, "It's a long shot, but the Royal Ontario Museum is at times looking for stockmen with a knowledge of geology, Why not see if they would be interested?"

I gave him all the cash I had and said, "This will get you a haircut and new clothes. Take with you my very best wishes."

"I don't know how to thank you," he said, "I'll be over at the Museum tomorrow. Here is something I want to give you." and he handed me a heavy plastic envelope, "Have a look at it when you get back to your room. I will never be able to get back there."

We shook hands, and I went back to the dormitory to reflect on the strange meeting triggered when I said, "May I join you?"

My buddies were hard at work, and asked what had happened to me? How was I going to make it as a geologist if I couldn't find my way two blocks up the street in Toronto?

I laughed, put the envelope in a drawer, and wondered what curious chance had brought me and the stranger together so we could talk without interruption. If I had been with the crowd there certainly would never have been the meeting between Mr. Wilkins and myself and I would never have heard his story, and there never would have been the effects of that strange story on so many lives in a far-away place. I could not have guessed that Mr. Wilkins and his small plastic package were to be the opening scene of a drama as unimaginable as anything that ever came from the imagination of the Greek dramatists.

With the examinations pressing hard, I forgot about Mr.Wilkins and his plastic envelope until it was all over and I was packing my things to go home.

CHAPTER TWO

Looking at the plastic envelope, I remembered how it had been easy to check on Arthur Wilkins. As I suspected, he had been in the class of 42.

Mom and Dad were due to pick me up in an hour and take me home. They had a nice place in Brampton and I was looking forward to home and a nice holiday until the examination results were published.

We played a lot of golf, swam in the pool and really had a nice holiday. One Thursday I came in from the pool just before lunch to see Mom and Dad hovering over a loaded table with Dad opening a bottle of bubbly.

"Bubbly at this hour? Must be a feast day or a holy day I have forgotten. Am I included?"

"A celebratory day of great significance. The Globe & Mail has published the examination results and you have the honor of being third in the Dean's Honor List. That's what the bubbly is about."

"Then I had better have a large glass to wash away the memories of endless hours of slaving in the library."

So we had our own celebration on that glorious day in May. Mom and Dad recalled the days when they were students at the University. Both had finished during the war and had immediately put on a uniform. After a simple wartime marriage Dad went overseas and Mom waited anxiously for my arrival.

Mom then invited the neighbors over for a pool party, and we had a delightful afternoon spiced up a bit by a neighbor lady and her two marriageable daughters, one of which had obviously been instructed to make herself visible to me. She did so in the smallest bikini I had ever seen. Her mother was fishing for an invitation for her daughter to the formal dinner of the class of 62 at the King Edward Hotel.

Mom had been watching the operation with an amused smile and then rescued me by sending me in to get cold beer for the guests.

Later that evening, Dad and I were sitting in the living room listening to Mom play some of her favorite Chopin nocturnes on the piano when I was suddenly jolted by a picture of the small map that Mr. Wilkins had drawn during that lunch we had shared. It flashed into my mind almost as if one had held the sketch in front of my face. But of course there was no one there. Strange. What could have brought that picture so sharply into focus at this particular moment?

Next morning, I took the plastic envelope out of the drawer. I opened the envelope, checked the notes I had made of our conversation, and opened the sealed envelope that Mr. Wilkins had given me. Inside was a heavy folded white paper. When I unfolded it I was astounded to see the original of the map that had flashed into my mind the evening before.

There was no question about the accuracy of the picture that had flashed into my mind–it was a precise replica of the map I had opened for the first time a few moments before. I could think of no explanation. I would have to have a hard look at this matter, but where to start? If I told Mom and Dad about this they would just tell me I was tired after the long grind in university and to forget it.

There was no doubt in my mind about this curious matter. The flash of the map that had appeared the evening before was an accurate picture of a map I had never seen. How could this be? Once more, the stories of the ancient Greek dramatists came to mind. What unseen and unknown force was guiding me? It could not be ignored.

Every geologist knows quite a lot about maps and cartography. I remembered that the Royal Canadian Air Force had done a splendid job of photographing all of Canada. These photographs would be on file in the archives of the Energy, Mines and Resources Department in Ottawa and certainly open to the public.

I made up a story about a possible interest in further studies in the field of cartography and booked a flight to Ottawa.

I arranged a grid on a small-scale map so I had an area to work through. There had been enough customer traffic looking at these photographs for the wizards at the cartographic section to have established a simple Ground Positioning System (GPS) overlay.

In two days of careful stereoscopic examination, I had

two possible locations. Each had a lake at the conjunction of two rivers, an advantage for landing a twin Otter on floats.

I was a bit apprehensive about going into this area alone, but did not know anyone I could trust to take along. Wild animals could be a problem, but the outfitters now had an array of quick response incendiary fireworks that would scare off any animal. I put a box of these in with my pistol, and then got all my camping gear organized for the trip.

My prospecting venture was going to be in Quebec so I carefully reviewed the regulations covering the staking of claims in that province. My French was not good enough to find my way through all the rules and regulations–if I found anything my first stop had better be a good bilingual lawyer familiar with the whole field. But first things first, I decided to go see if the map had any validity.

I took commercial air to Quebec City, and then got a charter twin Otter to drop me at my GPS position.

All went well, but I did notice that the pilot seemed to be curious about what I was looking for, so I told him I was working for the Iron Ore Company, as there were indications of iron and copper in the region. He soon lost interest, and after dropping me at the lakeshore he said, "You should have fine fish dinners up here."

"I'll be out there in the Zodiac as soon as I'm unpacked, and have my tent set up."

"Good luck, and I'll see you back here at about this time in three days."

He taxied out into deeper water, and took off down the lake disappearing into the sky. A great silence settled around me. I moved farther away from where animals might come down to the lake for a drink, then set up my tent before gathering enough large stones to build a fireplace. There was a good supply of deadwood close at hand.

When the Zodiac was inflated, I took my fishing rod and tackle box, and paddled out into deep water, feeling like a schoolboy on holiday. I dropped my baited hook overboard, and it took about one minute for a strike. I reeled it in, and had a respectable three-pound trout. I threw it back in, and tossed my hook and bait out once more. In a couple of minutes there was another pull on the line, so I reeled it in. About four pounds, I guessed.

Back to shore, I cleaned the fish and built my fire. The fillets filled the frying pan. Thirty minutes from lake to my dinner plate–can't get much better than that.

I dropped the food residue into the lake and watched it disappear, almost in seconds. The lake was full of hungry fish. A nice trout would be splendid for an early breakfast.

I checked my compass. The early morning sun would give me full light on the various sediment layers on the escarpment across the lake, and I wanted to make the most of that. It was only about two hundred yards across the arm of the lake to where I would start my climb to see if this was the location of the cave on Mr. Wilkins' map, and the location of the bonanza he spoke about.

It was beginning to shade into dusk, so I stoked up my fire, as best I could, and set my alarm clock to awaken me in three hours to replenish the logs on the fire. I put two of my incendiary fireworks near the tent door, placed my pistol close by and crawled into my sleeping bag. The place was as silent as could be, and as I fell asleep I hoped it would remain so all night.

The alarm woke me, and I thought I heard movement outside the tent. I opened the door and could smell the rancid odor of animal but whatever it was, it was happy to be gone. I rebuilt the fire and went back to sleep thinking about what a marvelous place this would be to build a lodge for summer fishing holidays.

My alarm woke me as the first morning light was creeping across the lake, and once again it took about two minutes to catch a decent trout for breakfast. It would be good with coffee and hardtack biscuits. I carefully cleaned up, strapped on my pistol, put an incendiary flare in my packsack and climbed into the Zodiac to paddle my way across the lake to begin my career as a geologist.

It was to be a short career. I climbed up the layers of the crumbling escarpment. Everything was as described by Mr. Wilkins. The shrubs hiding the cave had grown in the intervening years, but since they were not based in a generous layer of soil, the growth had been slow. I could see the large rock ahead so made as little noise as possible. When I got into position behind it I listened for animal noise. With my pistol in my hand, I peeked around the corner. Nothing. I picked up a small rock and threw it into the cave, and waited for a response. Again nothing.

I had brought a large powerful flashlight so I turned it on, and slowly went around the big rock where I could shine the light into the cave. There was a terrible animal smell, but nothing moved, and I shone the light from side to side to make sure it was empty. Again nothing moved, so I ventured in. There did not seem to be any fresh droppings. I ran the light over the floor of the cave, and got reflections from gold nuggets lying about.

It took me about an hour to select a variety of nuggets. It would be all I could carry without attracting attention. I added a good layer of iron ore samples and copper oxide chunks, in case anyone wanted to look into my sample bag.

Next, I took a series of pictures of the layers visible on the wall of the cave. There seemed to be one of solid gold and about two inches thick running around the whole cave. I could hardly believe my eyes.

Putting in my claim stakes was a problem. They had to be visible, but not too much so. I checked and rechecked the GPS locations so there could be no dispute about the claim boundaries, and then I went back across the lake to my campsite.

The full impact of the find had not really sunk into my brain. How could I, or anyone else put a realistic value on the visible gold or the assess that might be found in the deeper layers of the escarpment–only a geologist experienced in gold mining could make an educated guess at that value. I could ask for a reasonable amount up front, but what about the value that would only be revealed in a couple of years of operation of the mine? If that non-visible value continued in the lower layers, the shares in the company would rise rapidly with each annual report. By the end of year two of operation the shares would have stabilized and I would either be an even richer man or I would have nice new uninteresting wallpaper.

The campsite was undisturbed, and I realized that I was hungry now after the morning's venture. I started a fire, put my equipment away in the tent, and went out in the

Zodiac to get another decent fish for a lunch.

Another quiet night, and then it was time to get ready for the arrival of the twin Otter to take me back to Quebec City. It was the same pilot. We loaded my equipment and made everything ready for take off. The sky was clear as far as the eye could see and as we flew along I got gentle enquiries from the pilot. He seemed to know about mines and mineral deposits, so I made a big thing out of bringing my sample bag forward and showing him the samples of iron ore and copper oxide. He recognized them instantly and quickly lost interest.

Back in Quebec City I paid off the charter, got my gear into a cab, and went to the airport to arrange a flight back to Toronto. I took one sample of the iron ore and one of the copper oxide, put everything else in a luggage lock-up and then made my way to the claims registry office. These things seemed to be routine and once again they lost interest when I gave them my two samples for assay.

I went back to the airport and called Dad at his office asking if he could enquire among his colleagues about a reliable law firm that knew their way around the mining business, and secondly could he make contact with a good, well established mining company that was in the gold mining business.

Dad picked me up at Pearson airport and we went home to Brampton. Dad poured us each an honest drink. Mom had food ready, so we relaxed and then we sat in the living room. I told them the whole story. They were wide-eyed at the sight of the gold nuggets in my sample bag.

Our next step was to get the whole matter under the protection and guidance of a good lawyer.

Dad said, "Look, I've been playing golf for years with the man you can trust to keep you safe in those shark infested waters of the mining industry. I'll see if he can make time for us tomorrow afternoon and we can get this thing tidied up"

We arrived at two pm, Dad introduced me, and Mr. Phillips looked at me expectantly.

"I've registered a claim in the province of Quebec, about an hour by air from Quebec City, I have samples I'd like you to see."

He looked carefully at the claim registration and said, "Seems to be neat and tidy, can we see the samples?"

I opened the sample bag and began to lay out the nuggets I had brought back. When I had finished he looked as if he couldn't believe what he was seeing. It took him a few minutes to gather his wits, and then he said, "The man you need to talk to right away is the Vice President of Maverick Gold Mining. Their offices are in this building on the 20th floor. May I call him and see if he can come down?"

"Of course."

He pressed his intercom button and asked his secretary to see if she could get George Watkins of Maverick on the phone urgently. Three minutes later the phone rang.

He pressed his speakerphone button so we could all hear,

"Its George, What's up?"

"Could you possibly come down to my office for a few minutes. I have something you really must see"

He was down five minutes later, was introduced to Dad and I, and then he caught sight of the nuggets lying on the lawyer's desk.

"My God, I've never seen anything like this in my life." He looked at Dad, and then at me, and back at the nuggets again.

"Can I get a couple of my boys down here to have a look at this display?"

"Of course."

When they had had a look at the nuggets I produced the photographs of the floor of the cave with the light reflecting off of the nuggets, and then showed them the photographs of the gold layer running around the wall of the cave. There was a long silence as they digested this information. Then the boss man looked at me and said, "I assume this is yours. What are you asking for the claim?"

"One million in an account in the Bank of Nova Scotia here in Toronto, six million U.S. in a Swiss account in my name, and fifty thousand preferred shares for each of the first two years of your operations on this site."

He looked at me for a moment before he said, "Would you like to come and work for me?"

"I'm flattered but I'm going to draw unemployment insurance for a while and maybe travel a bit."

"My Board of Directors would perform a rude operation on me if I didn't have a look before I signed. How soon can we do this?"

"Do you have a good sized aircraft on floats with a pilot who is your employee?"

"Yes."

I looked at the lawyer and asked, "Can you draw up all the papers ready for final signature this afternoon?"

"Bit of a hurry but yes."

"Let me make a suggestion. If your aircraft and pilot, and the whole lot of us plus, a security team can be ready tomorrow morning, we can leave then. They should be prepared to camp out there for a few days. We can all go to the site. It's about two hours flying time. Bring bags for collecting nuggets for your meeting with the Board of Directors."

I looked at Dad. He nodded his agreement. The lawyer nodded so I said, to the Mining boss, "Where and when do we meet? By the way we will be in wild animal country if any of you have any side arms bring them along. Your security boys will know what to do. There is a splendid camping place for them to set up shop."

The mining boss came to Dad and I, and said, "Were you joking about extra bags?"

"No, you will have a bag full of nuggets in half an hour."

We met at Pearson next morning at six am. Everyone seemed as excited as schoolboys going out on a day's exploration.

Still not trusting anyone, I gave the pilot a GPS position ten minutes south of our real destination for his flight plan, and we took off. An hour out, I gave the pilot the correction.

On arrival he flew low over what would be his landing run to make sure there were no floating logs, and then he came around again and landed. He taxied over to what had been my campsite, and they started to unload their gear.

We inflated the Zodiac, and the five of us climbed in, leaving the security chaps to do their thing while we went across the lake, and made our way up the escarpment to the cave. As we came closer to the entrance of the cave, I cautioned them and went forward to get a rock and threw it into the cave to see if there was any response.

All was silent, but the smell of animals and their droppings was almost overpowering. We turned on our flashlights and stepped into the cave. As the lights moved around on the floor, the reflections of the many nuggets shone back at us. I heard the mining boss say softly "My God", and then he went to the wall of the cave to look at the layer of gold reflecting light back to us. He followed the layer around, and then stepped back and began to pick nuggets from the floor. Ten minutes later he said, "I'm ready to go back home."

We made our way back to the Zodiac and then to the other side of the lake where the security fellows now had their tents up and a fire going.

"The lake is teeming with hungry lake trout. Five minutes fishing will get you enough fish for a first class lunch for all of us. I'll help you with catching and filleting, if you like."

There was no great need to hurry to get back so everyone just sat back and waited for their plateful of fish to come off of the pan.

Then it was time to go back home.

When we were heading back to Toronto I saw the mining boss take out his bag of nuggets and carefully examine them one by one. Then he turned to me and said, "I sure wish I could persuade you to come and work for me. I need people like you. What are you going to do now?"

"I've had two passionate dreams since I was a teenager. I want to spend time traveling all over France to absorb the history of the past ten centuries. I also want to have a small ranch with a pure bred Black Angus beef herd."

"You are going to abandon geology?"

"I think so."

"Well, if you do ranching like you do geology I'll make sure my wife buys all her beef from your ranch."

When we got close to Toronto, Dad called Mom and said, "It's celebration night back at the homestead. Fillet mignon and bubbly please."

My first call the next day would be to see if the lawyer could make contact with Mr. Arthur Wilkins and tell him he had just become a millionaire.

CHAPTER THREE

It was June 4th, 1962, and I was on my way to Le Harve from Paris. I had arrived at Orly and decided to spend a few days in Paris before picking up my car, a rather nice Peugeot 105, and had decided to crisscross France from west to east. I had a full complement of road maps and Michelin Guides.

I wanted to be back in Paris for the Bastille Day to see what the national holiday celebrations were about. I had lots of time and made my way through the calvados country, the World War Two points of the invasion, and then through the World War One memorials. It was an interesting challenge trying to keep the earlier French-English wars, and then the Napoleonic battlefields in their particular context.

The Michelin Guides were invaluable so I lazily poked my way through the countryside from LeHavre to Verdun, and then back to Paris by the tenth of July to get more familiar with the city before Bastille Day brought all its celebrations.

A serious student of cathedral architecture could spend more time than I had on the cathedrals alone. The stained glass windows were breathtaking, especially the red ones at St. Stephens in northern Paris. It was all very exciting for a tourist like me coming from the rather scant history we had in the province of Ontario.

Those weeks in northern France nicely set the scene for the tour through the Loire Valley. So I waved farewell to Fontainbleu and I set off for Anger and the wonders of the Loire Valley.

It was like a fairy tale with many chapters. I wondered about the lives of those aristocrats as they spent the seasons at Chambord or Chenonceau away from Paris. Once again, my small knowledge of engineering surfaced, as it had at Mont St. Michel. I marveled at the capacity of the builders to move those huge quantities of stone needed for the construction.

It was now the middle of August, and as I drove down the main highway toward Marseilles and the south of France I thought about spending the next two weeks down on the Riviera playgrounds before I went back to Canada. In September winter would not be far away and I had never really like winter.

As I drove past the vineyards and green fields I wondered if these people ever experienced snow and zero temperature for weeks on end. Truth to tell, if I never saw another snowstorm I wouldn't miss them.

I left the main highway, at a village miles north of where I would have to make a decision on whether to go straight to the grubby, busy port, or turn eastwards to the Riviera. As I was having lunch I asked myself if I really wanted another Canadian winter or did I want to spend those months in the warm sunshine.

The name of Mr. Wilkins popped into my head as I was having lunch, and I wondered what he had decided to do when he received the cheque for one million dollars. Next time I spoke to the lawyer I would remember to ask if he knew.

Lunch finished, I filled the gasoline tank knowing I had made my decision to explore the coastal area, and to leave the city until later. So, I drove down to where the main highway turned eastward, and once more I marveled at the vineyards and the luxurious green fields. Back home most of the farmland would have been denuded of the crops and getting ready for the onset of fall and winter.

About eight kilometers on, I came to a sleepy old village set back a short distance from the highway. The old road ran right in front of the village, and then back to join the main highway again. It was an old cobblestone road, with an asphalt surface. An old Roman road? The village was nestled on flatland at the base of a ridge of hills covered with a splendid forest.

I drove slowly through the village and noted that all the buildings were made of a stone cut in rather larger sizes than one sees nowadays. There were cottages, a few two story houses, shops, and what seemed to be a community and public office building with the French flag flying from a flagstaff. I drove back to where I had entered the village to look at the collection of ruined buildings.

I noticed the "A Vendre" sign, and parked the car and walked around. Why were these abandoned? Did an aristocrat find himself on the losing side in one of the many wars, and lose his property and his head as a result? I noticed that someone, and obviously quite some time ago, from the overgrowth, had invested quite a lot of labor in recovering the stones from the outbuildings. Why had they stopped? Why was the place for sale now?

I slowly drove back to the community building, parked, and went inside. There was a young lady, receptionist and tourist information guide, who spoke English.

Yes, the property was for sale. It was purchased four years ago by a retired American couple. They had wanted to build a modern home with the old stone, but months after they began, he had a heart attack and died. She went back to her home in the United States."

"How much land is there in the whole property?" I asked.

"The real estate agent is in his office on the second floor. May I call him and ask him to come down to give you any information you would like?"

"I would be most grateful."

The agent's English was as limited as my French so we asked the young lady if she would act as translator for us. She smiled and said that she would be happy to be able to practice.

There were one hundred and ten hectares of land in the property.

It had belonged to an old aristocratic family, who found themselves on the wrong side of a war, and lost their heads as a result. It was now owned by the village authorities. No taxes had been paid on it for years.

"And what is the purchase price?

He did calculations on a piece of paper and then said, "I assume you are an American, so I have translated the French francs into American dollars–at today's rate of exchange the price would be $400,000.00.

"Does the price include everything on the property?"

"Of course."

"May I go back and have another look at the place? I will come back in an hour with a decision."

I thanked them, and went back to walk around the property. I wondered about the possibility of a source for water. I had not seen a well in my short trip around the ruins earlier, but now I found a bubbling spring at one end of the property at the base of the hill. A small rivulet ran around and down to a culvert underneath the road and beyond. It was clean, clear and cool. It was perfect and would be ideal for household use, and for my herd of Black Angus cattle.

I returned to the office and said, that I would take the property, and we could arrange to close the sale next day or as soon as convenient for them.

"Is there a place in the village where I might find a room and meals in the coming days?"

"At the end of the next street there is the Auberge Des Grenadiers. I will call them and ask them to take care of you. It is a quiet place, and they will be happy to have you."

I discovered, later that evening, that the inn was owned by the young lady's parents, and that her twin sister was the manager and waitress in the restaurant. I checked in and was shown a very nice comfortable room. I had scarcely finished unpacking my things when there was a knock on the door, and what I thought was the young lady from the recreation center. She handed me a small tray with a drink on it and said, " Dinner is served at six."

My surprise at seeing her must have been written all over my face so she laughed and said, "It was my twin sister you met this afternoon. I am Lisa. She is Giselle. I will take care of you while you are staying here with us. Please ask me for any help you need. Father saw your Canadian passport, and would like to welcome you with a drink of Canadian rye whiskey."

She smiled and was gone before I could say, thank you. It was twenty to six, so I washed up, finished my drink and went downstairs to be in time for dinner. Lisa showed me to a table and a moment later appeared with shrimps in horseradish sauce and a glass of white wine, then a plate of roast beef and vegetables. The chef and my mother could have come from the same school I thought. As I was finishing dessert the owner came in and said, "Since we are going to be neighbors we would like to invite you to join us for coffee and a brandy."

"I would be delighted, thank you"

After introductions and the brandy was poured, Mr. St.Onge told me that at the beginning of the war he had enlisted in the French Navy. It was shortly before the Admirals had decided to scuttle the battleships at Toulon. He and some of his mates had made their way in a stolen boat to Gibraltar, and then to joined the Free French Forces. Since there was no French navy, he had joined a British

Artillery unit.

The British had gathered a number of French escapees, put them in this unit, smuggled them in with the help of the French underground, and they had set up their guns in the rear of the German defenses and were ranged in as the first invasion troops hit the shores of Normandy.

It took the Germans a while to figure out what was happening, but by then it was too late as their reserves were held too far back, and the Allied air superiority created havoc.

When it was all over they marched down the main streets of Paris, and then he came back to his home to find his fiancé and to get on with their lives. He was curious about someone my age being able to produce the cash necessary to buy the property and to pay for the cost of rebuilding. Was I intending to live here permanently? Did I have a family who would come and live here in France? Was I some kind of farmer?

It was obvious that he needed a couple of sons-in-laws. They were astonished when I told them I was a geologist who had come out of the university that spring semester. I told them that my father was a stockbroker in the city, and my parents had no intention of leaving Canada.

I changed the subject, and asked if he knew an architect who could help me with the rules and regulations of the region, and who would find a competent construction company to get the building program underway.

He couldn't make any sense out of my being a geologist and wanting to raise a herd of pure bred Black Angus cattle. He did know a very good architect in the next town, seven kilometers farther east. If I were prepared to drive, he would ask Lisa to go along as a guide and deliver a note of introduction. It was obvious that Lisa and I were going to become better acquainted. I would have to be careful. The bait was attractive.

Lisa had shopping to do, but could she be back at the office in time for lunch? We could and went to a nice place. I noticed the architect, a relatively young man, paying a good deal of attention to Lisa. The trip back was pleasant, as I had bought a large bouquet of flowers as a thank you to Lisa for her help. All I could do now was wait for the contractor to get in motion, and on the clearing up and the recovery of usable stone.

CHAPTER FOUR

It took two days to get a clean up crew on the site and two weeks to get all the demolition work done. During this time, I worked very closely with the architect in getting the curious design features I wanted, but since there was no noise from me about keeping costs down he went along to see where my design ideas would carry us. He had obviously never met a fellow who wanted to play around with flower gardens and Black Angus cattle before, so it seemed to be a learning process for him as well as for me.

I had been curious for years, about the energy that a simple pyramid produces. Little was known in the engineering faculty in the University of Toronto, and there seemed to be very little research published. I was intrigued by what I had been able to turn up and determined to experiment with this when I was able to do so. How did exposure to that pyramid energy affect flowers, water, food, and so on. How much exposure was needed? My roses and strawberries would come first.

By mid-December, I was living in a house that needed a lot of fine finishing work. The swimming pool was finished, my botanist's hothouse was ready for my beginning experiments with crossing roses, the fences had been upgraded, and my first six Black Angus cattle were on their new range.

I wanted to take ten days off and go back home to spend Christmas with Mom and Dad. On the flight home I thought about the fellow who had been my best buddy during the high school days. He was one of four sons of a German immigrant couple who lived in Brampton. The father had been trained as a finishing carpenter in Germany and brought a real genius to everything he did. He had carefully trained the boys in all the basic skills as they grew up, and they just blended into the business when they left high school. I wondered if I could get my friend Klaus to come over for a three or four months working holiday and do things for me. It would be worth a try.

I looked Klaus up over the Christmas holidays and told him and his father what I had been doing in France, and I asked him if he would be interested in coming over, for two or three months, to help with the finishing work. His father said that things were slow in the house building business in winter and why would he not go. He would have a much-needed holiday at the same time. Little could either his father or I have guessed at the outcome of his visit. But more of that later.

We came to France together after the New Year's celebration had died down, and we set up a workshop for him in the garage. His first major task was to build and mount the many pyramids I wanted in the kitchen and in the wine and food storage cabinets. The botany workshop would be next and then the decorative work.

A few days after we had gotten settled, Lisa and her father came over one morning to wish me a Happy New Year. We chatted at the pool for a few minutes and then went into the kitchen for coffee. Klaus was there and turned around as we entered. I started to introduce him to the visitors, but I was startled at what was happening between Lisa and Klaus. Not a word had been spoken, but the electricity passing between them was almost visible. It was as if they were completely unaware of Mr. St. Onge and myself. I looked at Mr. St Onge. He looked at me as if he was telling me that he had now found the first son-in-law he wanted. Lisa broke the silence and gave Klaus her hand and a bright, "How do you do."

After lunch I called Madam St. Onge to see if I could make a reservation for dinner for two that evening. She had better get into the picture as soon as possible. I didn't want to think of a future for the St. Onge family without Lisa.

It didn't take Madam St. Onge long to get sharply in

focus. Klaus and I were invited into their sitting room for coffee and brandy after our dinner. Klaus, of course, could see nothing but Lisa, but I had the distinct feeling that I was watching him get measured for his wedding suit. I was trying to imagine what Klaus' family back in Brampton would say.

Two days later, I got my first indicator of what was on the horizon. Klaus came to me and said that he had been talking to his family on the phone the night before and had asked if one of his brothers could be spared for a couple of months to come over and help him as there was a great deal of work to be done, and he had noted that there was a good deal of work around the St. Onge inn that needed doing. He thought it was a marvelous place, and with imaginative changes could be turned into a wonderful tourist stop.

"Would your brother Robert come over for a while? How busy are they?"

"It is winter in Ontario and finishing work is mostly waiting for the arrival of spring and the new house owners' market to start buzzing. Robert would like to come. By the way, when you were gone to Marseilles the other day the mayor of the village came and asked if he could see the large wall map I was making. He could hardly believe what he saw, and then asked if when I was finished here could I make a large map of France for the council chamber."

"Tell Robert that his flight tickets will be lodged with the Air France office at Pearson this afternoon. He can make arrangements to suit himself, and we can pick him up at the airport here in Marseilles on arrival. When you and Robert have a few moments would you like to look at the council chamber the mayor was talking about and see what we can do. It might be a nice gift to the village. Don't tell him that. There probably is an ancient colorful crest hidden in the village history, left over from the days when knights were galloping around on horseback. It could be resurrected, adopted by the local authorities, and put on the entrance wall of the community centre. It certainly would catch the eyes of any tourists who came wandering into the place."

There was one rather conspicuous feature to this small delightful village set at the bottom of a hill. Perhaps it was just my Canadian eye that saw this. It was the absence of trees. I recalled the magnificent, stately redwood trees we had seen out west, and thought that the curved line at the bottom of the hill needed some of these–about two hundred. I wondered what regulations the Government of France had about importing foreign species and planting them. Well, I would soon enough find out.

CHAPTER FIVE

The weeks sped by quickly. Our loose corporate structure was taking shape. George Charboneau, the clever architect, had come up with a stroke of genius in the design for the inn. Similar in shape, different in size, it presented a view of the village that made it look as if it had come from the brush of a master painter. Re-named the Auberge St.Onge, it caught the eye of tourists as the village was nestled in the flatland just below the ridge of hills. George was now busy with the new homes for the newly weds. They had decided to build these houses around a quadrangle behind the auberge, so that when the children came there would be convenience for the mothers.

However, a new factor had entered the equation. When Klaus was married his parents came over and were delighted with the place and surprised to find the exquisite woodworking that Klaus and Robert had done in the village.

Firstly the exquisite large map of the world on the wall

in my house, then the map of France, and the village crest in the community centre, and now the interior of the Auberge.

Klaus and Robert were continually being surprised by the requests they were getting from sources in the surrounding country. They could be busy for at least two years with orders if they wished to accept them.

Mrs. St.Onge's sister, and her daughter, Denise, had come to live with the St.Onge family, and became part of the staff. Denise would finish her course at the University. She was an attractive young lady, and three years younger than her twin cousins, Lisa and Giselle, and everyone around the place could see that she and Robert were going to make a future together. George would have to build another house.

Lisa called me one morning and said, there had been a problem with the bus to the city and Denise needed a ride to get registered and established at the University. Could I please help? So Denise and I collected her luggage and left for Marseilles. I accompanied her to the Registration office and while I was waiting I noticed a poster advertising a two semester program for a Master of Business Administration– given in English, one half day per week. I enquired. Yes I could register. I would be student number seventeen in the course. First lecture on Wednesday, September 3rd, from 10: am to 1 pm. I found all the textbooks and course material at the Book Shop and then went for lunch

Back home, I examined the course outline. Each student was expected to give a two hour seminar on an industry problem; first an outline of the significance of the problem, and then the solution in detail.

They package included a list of the names of the students registered–eight engineers, mostly French graduates–three American Arts bachelors–four with certification unknown to me, probably refugees from the Communist world, and one M.Sc. Ph.D. from the University of British Columbia. The last should be a heavyweight to watch in action.

I would have to review the selected subjects carefully, and get my selection approved for the first meeting, as it would probably be a scramble in a group like this.

George had finished building the houses for the newly weds, and Klaus and Lisa moved out of my guest room and into their new home. George had been sensible and done a really first class job of the design work and they were models of stone houses–after all he and Giselle were going to spend much of their lives in one of them.

I asked George one day, "Have you given any thought to what the corporation should do about Robert and Denise. It certainly looks as if another house will be required in the village?"

"Yes. I have discussed, with Klaus, the possibility of setting up a new company, with offices here in the village, named simply Charboneau, Leitman. It would handle all aspects of construction. He would be pleased indeed to do so, but he said rather plainly, that we had better include Robert because he was critical to the woodworking contracts already spoken for, and secondly that it looked as if he was going to become a member of the family. The girls are already talking about the wedding plans."

" Does the corporation need more funding?"

I had called Mom and Dad two nights earlier and been

told that Maverick Gold was now selling at $120.00 per share. It was probably peak price, so I had asked Dad to sell my shares and deposit the money in my Swiss account. Robert had been quietly working very hard for long hours without ever making a complaint and it was time for payback.

"Do you think we should get Klaus into the act and get Robert into a discussion on becoming a partner in the firm so he can have a solid financial base for proposing to Denise?"

Robert could hardly have been more delighted when we laid the proposition out for him that evening. He said, "I know Mom and Dad are going to be disappointed at losing another of their sons to the village, but I feel that my future is here with Denise, and I think she feels the same."

"Look, I don't want to sound like an interfering busybody but I do like to get things nailed down properly. I'm going into Marseilles tomorrow, so why don't you come with me to a jewelry shop I know, and then we can have a pool party this weekend and you can make your announcement."

"I don't have enough money for a ring," Robert said.

"Oh yes you do, your credit within the corporation is much greater than you know. All of this can be sorted out later on. Can you be ready about eight?"

When we got to the jewelry shop and Robert started looking at engagement rings I noticed he was startled at the prices of diamonds so I said, "You are only going to do this once. Remember the money can always be replaced but the girl cannot. Lisa and Giselle are wearing rings that look like they are about two carats. You do not want Denise to feel that she cannot be equally proud of hers in the months and years to come. Don't worry about the money."

Then to the jeweler, "Lets start looking at two carats."
We settled on a square cut two and a half carat engagement
ring that was part of a locking engagement and wedding
ring set, the wedding ring studded with small diamonds.
Robert just shook his head, but I was thinking of Denise's
reaction.

On the way home I said, to Robert, " George wants to
create a separate arm of the corporation in a company that
will deal with all construction. As you know he has already
done the houses for Klaus and himself. There is space on
the other side of the quadrangle for another house, and he
would like to get plans drawn up. We would like to blend
you and Denise into the working team that is the
corporation. We should also blend Denise and you into the
larger family. After you and Denise have announced your
engagement would you talk to George about what you want
in your house."

"I just can't absorb all this on such short notice.
Yesterday I was wondering if I could ever ask Denise to
marry me, and today every problem has been swept away. I
can hardly believe what you have told me, but I sure as hell
am going to move on your suggestions."

"We are going to have an afternoon pool party on
Saturday, with the St.Onge mother and father, Mrs.
St.Onge's sister, Klaus and Lisa, and George and Giselle.
Denise is coming home this weekend and, of course, you
will be the star of the weekend show. You should speak to
the St. Onge mom and dad and Denise's mother about your
intentions and ask for their approval. Have a pretty speech
available for an occasion that we will all remember."

Saturday rolled around and like most days was warm and sunny, ideal for a pool party. Everyone was happy and had a few glasses of wine when Mr. St. Onge rang the bell and said he had an announcement to make.

"It is my great pleasure to be able to announce the engagement of Denise and Robert. They plan to marry as soon as her course of studies is over in the spring, and they will live here in the village."

We broke out the champagne and everyone was happy to have such a fine reason to celebrate.

September rolled around, and with it came the first class of my new venture into the academic world.

Seventeen of us gathered and took a seat in the room. I was surprised to find myself sitting two rows behind what seemed to be an oriental young lady. When the professor arrived he asked us to stand and introduce ourselves and to my surprise again the oriental lady stood up and said, simply "Patricia Quinn."

This was the heavy weight Ph.D. in the class and I wondered what strange circumstance had brought her from Vancouver to an MBA class in Marseilles.

We all did our thing and then came the business of assigning topics for the seminars, and I wondered how the professor was going to handle the problem of who would be first and second in their seminar presentations. He asked for volunteers and got a long silence in response and then Patricia Quinn raised her hand.

"Thank you, and your selected topic for the seminar?

" Cultural aspects of crime among immigrant communities and community responses."

Not a trace of an accent, it could easily be any

Canadian girl speaking. She seemed to be rather attractive, but there was nothing about her clothing that would catch anyone's eye. She was, either very bright, or older than she looked. Probably born in Canada and certainly she'd been educated in Canada. Her seminar might reveal other information.

The professor announced that due to space allocation problems our seminars would take place in the afternoons, from two to five pm, same place. Was this going to cause any problems for any of us?

I was to give the fourth seminar so I was interested to see how high our Chinese lady set the bar in her first presentation. Well, I might have been concerned. Her presentation was flawless, fine-tuned and loaded with statistical data. Obviously she had done her thesis in this area of study. I was going to have to get busy to even be in the ballpark.

When she was finished and asked for questions, there were one or two and then I thought I should lead in giving her a fine round of applause for the work she had done. She looked startled at first and then gave us all a big smile and a thank you.

Since the café was in the same building as our classroom I had taken to going there for an hour after class to get thing to eat and kill a bit of time until the heavy traffic on the main road cleared. On a few occasions, I had noticed that our Chinese lady, Patricia Quinn, would also come to the café and sit off in a corner reading a book while she had thing to eat.

One day, after our mid February seminar, I was in the café getting ready to wrap up my books and get ready to leave when Miss Quinn came up to the table and asked me, in rather a loud voice if I had a reference the professor had given us in class. As she did so, she put a note on the table in front of me. It said, 'Please help me. Those two Chinese men sitting over by the exit are going to kidnap me when I leave the café.'

"Yes, I have the reference. Please sit down it will take me a few minutes to find it, and I will write it out for you." I dug a couple of books, and a notepad out of my backpack and wrote her a note

'Wait 15 minutes after I leave and then take your purse and go to the washroom behind that floral screen. Next to the washroom doors is a door to the kitchen. Go through it, and then go out the back door into the alleyway. Turn left to the main street. A red convertible will be waiting.'

I finished writing the note, gave it to her and said, "That should get you the information you need. See you next week."

I picked up my things and the check, and went to the cashier, paid the bill, and went out to the parking lot. I was mystified at this turn of events, but she did look frightened.

I parked at the corner, and a minute later she appeared and quickly got into the car. We went off to join the highway, and then home where we might sort this problem out.

As we reached the main highway, I could see that she was crying silently and then she said, "I'm sorry to do this to you but I had no one else to turn to."

"Never mind, you are safe now and we can talk about the problem when we get home."

I drove along as quickly as I could checking the rear

view mirror from time to time to see if we were being followed. Nothing. When we arrived, I showed her where the bathroom was and said that I would pour a drink for her while I made thing to eat. When she joined me in the kitchen she said, "You live here all alone?"

"Yes. An outcast, unloved, unwanted, motherless child, a pariah in the community."

Then, for the first time, I saw the serious look on her face change and she gave me a smile that lit up the room. I marveled at the change in her. We sat at the table and ate shrimp in hot sauce and sipped our wine until the steaks were defrosted and then I braised them and mixed up my favorite Stilton cheese in potato mixture. We discovered how hungry we were over a glass of red wine. She ate as if she hadn't had a decent meal in a week. Then we cleaned up the kitchen and took a cup of coffee and cookies into the living room, sat down and then I said, "Now please tell me the whole story."

" Mom and Dad came to Vancouver as immigrants from Hong Kong at the end of the depression. Things were very hard apparently, and they finally started a small convenience store and through a lot of hard work made it grow into a thriving business. They had three daughters. I am number two. My older sister has two children. Her husband was killed in a construction accident two years ago. She and the children live at home and she works in the store.

Five years ago one of the tongs in Hong Kong decided to get established in the Chinese community in Vancouver. The boss of the tong, a polished, ruthless, murderous thug visited all the business people in the community. They were going to help them by protecting them from the oppressive laws and regulations that the civic authorities were laying on them, but this protection was going to cost the business people a little money from time to time. You have probably heard of this extortion racket before.

I was in my last year of high school at the time and was helping in the store when the tong delegation came to see my Dad. The boss of the tong seemed to be taken with me, and in the discussion with Dad he proposed that he and I get married. He assured my father that things could go very well for him if he agreed to the marriage and father said that he would only consider it after I had finished my education. There was no terminal date and as soon as high school was finished I enrolled in the university.

I enjoyed the challenges and was seventeen when I first started at UBC. My proposed marriage was put on hold, but when I enrolled in a graduate program three years later he knew he was being stalled by father and started to make things difficult. The protection fees increased, and when father objected he had an accident in the store. It was no accident, of course, but it warned us of things to come.

Two years later when I was finishing my thesis there was an ugly scene between father and him and not long after that there was a robbery in the store, and father was killed.

Mother was convinced the tong had done it but with no proof she could do nothing. She managed to sell the business, and we moved to a house in the suburbs. But you know how the Chinese are about "face". He was the head of the tong and determined to have me as the wife he had been bragging about for years. I was equally determined that I would never marry him, and shortly after I finished my thesis at UBC I saw an ad in the Economist magazine for this MBA program here in Marseilles.

Hoping I would be out of the way and safe, half a world away I disappeared from Vancouver. Face was important to him, and two weeks ago he turned up here and was waiting for me after I got home from class one evening. He had long owned a 60 foot motorized yacht, and he and two of his henchmen had come through the Panama Canal to the Azores and then to Marseilles. They had followed me home from class and then a few days later had entered my apartment and stolen my passport.

When class was over today, I went to the café. I saw them sitting by the door waiting for me to leave/ They would just take me to the boat and back to Vancouver. The rest you know."

I could hardly credit this story but she had been frightened and I did see the two Chinese fellows sitting by the door in the café. I gathered our coffee cups and cleaned up the kitchen.

Klaus had long since moved out of my guest bedroom so she could sleep there and be comfortable while we decided what to do.

First she needed clothes and basics like a toothbrush. She couldn't go back to her apartment. They would be watching it. I said, to her, "There is a respectable department store in the next city, about fifteen kilometers east of here. Could we get away early tomorrow morning and get the things you will need?"

"I can't do that because I have only a few francs, and my bank book and money is in the apartment."

"Never mind about money, that can be sorted out later. We have to get you comfortable and think of how we are going to manage to keep you safe. They will be making every effort to find you and the obvious place to start is with the people you know, your classmates. It won't take them long to get here, I expect."

"I'll find you a toothbrush and a pair of my pajamas so you can get some sleep."

Next morning when I came down to the kitchen I found her sitting by the table drinking orange juice, looking lost and frightened.

"I trust you slept well," I said,.

"A night full of bad dreams. You have been lucky in never having come into contact with people like those tong members. They have a whole culture of their own and will stop at nothing. The laws mean nothing to them."

"Would you like fresh strawberries for breakfast?" I asked her.

She looked surprised, then smiled and said, "Yes, please."

I took a bowl and tongs and a small knife and then asked her to join me in the strawberry hunt. We went out to the nursery building and, in a few minutes had gathered a bowl full of large berries from the plants and took them back to the kitchen.

"Will you have yours in with your cereal?"

" Just berries, toast and coffee please."

I took a large, deep red strawberry, removed the hull and said, "Close your eyes and open your mouth," and popped the berry into her mouth. It was luscious and tasty and she smiled when she finished chewing it and looked as if she were more comfortable. I hoped that some of the ice had been broken.

We finished breakfast, cleaned up, and then made our way out of town to do some shopping. I found a personal shopping assistant and told her that Dr. Quinn had lost all her luggage so she needed everything. Please get her outfitted completely. Then I found a comfortable chair and a magazine to read.

There was a full page color picture, of a blonde woman with her two children, in the magazine. It occurred to me that I could easily get a frame, put this picture in it in a conspicuous place in the living room, so that if these fellows were to make their way into the house they would see it, and have an explanation for the women's things around the house.

" Just a small deception should they break into the house while we are away."

"What if they come while we are here? They do have guns, and have no hesitation about using them."

I had been wondering how we could throw her pursuers off track. What if she were to get a flight from Marseilles to Paris, and come right back to Marseilles by bus leaving no paper trail behind her? But there was the matter of her passport. Could she travel within the country without a passport, or identity papers?

Two nights later all our questions were answered. We had been watching a movie on TV and were late in going to bed. I had just turned the lights off, and set the alarm system on alert when the alarm system went off.

I checked the location of the problem and saw two people on the other side of the wall surrounding the swimming pool. I went to the wall, and saw someone coming over the top of the fence on a rope ladder. As he went to take the last step onto the patio I gave him a sharp blow on the back of the head, and he collapsed onto the floor without a sound. We tied his hands and feet with a cord, and put duct tape over his mouth to keep him quiet.

We waited to see what the other fellow was going to do. If all was silent would he come over as well or would he abandon the first one and leave?

Our answer was not long in coming. He came up over the wall as his colleague had done, and once more as he took the last step down I gave him a sharp blow on the head and he fell to the patio floor. We soon had him tied up and gagged.

I looked out front, and saw their rented van backed into the carport, so we put both of them into the back of the van and wondered what to do next.

" Lets just take them back to the marina near their boat and leave them for the other fellow to find them," I said, "but that doesn't solve the problem of your passport."

" Let us have a look at what they have on them by way of identification or other information."

We found their wallets and took them inside to see what they would reveal; a British Columbia driver's licence, a provincial health card, quit a lot of French money, and, in one pocket, a small paper with three figures; 8–15–27. It could only be the combination of a safe, and that is where the passport would be.

"If I drive the van back to the marina, can you identify their boat? We could repay their visit with one of our own. Can you drive my car and follow me there?"

"Yes."

As we slowly made our way along the line of boats at the marina I saw the name "The Chinese Girl", so I drove the van onto the jetty they used for loading, not noticing that the jetty was on an incline.

We parked the car, climbed onto the boat, and opened the door to the main cabin.

All I could hear was loud snoring, so we crept down to where the third fellow was keeping watch, but not much. He had a large alcoholic smell about him. I pointed to him, and she nodded, so I went over to the safe over in the corner. After a few minutes, I had it open, and there, on top of a leather briefcase, was a blue Canadian passport. A quick look told me it was hers, so I put it in the briefcase.
The papers were the ownership contract, and the insurance policy. Back into the safe with those things, they had no value for us. I took the briefcase, locked the safe, and we went out as quietly as we had come in.

As we got over the side of the boat, I noticed that the van was missing. I had left the key in it. Had someone come along and stolen it? A more likely possibility was that it had rolled down the incline and off of the end of the jetty, and was now at the bottom of two hundred feet of seawater.

We made our way back to my car, and as quietly as we could drove home. We both realized what had happened, but there was no proof so we could do nothing but await developments.

I gave Patricia her passport and threw the briefcase on my desk where I could have a look at it next day.

Patricia went to bed happy to have her passport once more, I reset the alarm system, but something nagged at the back of my mind telling me to have a look at the briefcase. I took it up to my bedroom, spread out the papers.

I found berthing approval certificates from the harbor authorities, and four certificates that I did not recognize–then I read the statement on the front of the certificate and realized I was looking at four American dollar bearer bonds, each worth one million dollars.

Our next seminar at the University was in four days and then we had one more to do to complete the course. We had better behave as normally as we could. As we went to the next class, we drove slowly past the line of boats at the marina and noticed that The Chinese Girl was gone.

I don't know what brought the thought to mind, but next morning I asked Patricia to call the harbormaster's office and enquire about the ship's departure and destination.

They advised her that they had no communication with any one on board. The ship had simply disappeared over night.

The next morning, when I went out to gather strawberries for breakfast I became aware of a new, or at least, hitherto unseen Patricia Quinn, If I had spent the years with her burden hanging around my neck I, too, might have felt like Coleridge's ancient mariner suddenly relieved of the albatross.

But there was another interesting twist to the story of "The Chinese Girl" that would appear a year and a half later.

CHAPTER SIX

Few things could be more repugnant than the threat of spending one's life as a servant of such a husband and Patricia's newfound sense of freedom and safety was easy to understand.

But, last night, when the significance of those four certificates came into focus, I could think of nothing better than pulling out the bottom drawer of my chest of drawers and putting the briefcase and four certificates on the floor beneath the drawer. There was no reason for anyone to be looking there. They would be safe until such time as it was possible to get them to my bank in Switzerland.

When "The Chinese Girl" vanished from her berth in the marina, and we could get no information from the harbormaster's office, we thought we had heard the last of the matter and went on with our lives.

How wrong we were. There was to be another strange

twist to the story months later. Curious indeed.

Patricia and I had just finished a late, lazy breakfast in the rose garden when the doorbell rang.

I found three distinguished looking, well dressed gentlemen there. One of them asked if Patricia Quinn was to be found at this address.

"Yes, she is, please come in."

Patricia came out and they introduced themselves

"James Truegood, assistant harbor master, Gibralter,"

"Alphonse Trecarten, assistant harbor master, at the port of Marseilles,"

"Jacques Carbotage, Attorney General's office in Paris."

They spoke excellent English and we chatted for a while until Patricia brought a tray with coffee and croissants, and then Mr. Trecarten opened the conversation.

"About a year and a half ago a yacht of Canadian registry named "The Chinese Girl" came into the port here and was berthed for two weeks. All the fees for the berth were paid up for a month, and then one night the ship disappeared from the marina and the harbor. We heard no more from her or about her until months later when she appeared in the harbor at Gibraltar. But let Mr. Truegood pick up the story from there".

"The ship had come into the harbor at Gibraltar, and then the engines were shut down. We called her a few times and all we could get by way of a reply was a faint "Mayday, Mayday."

We gathered a couple of paramedics, two policemen, and a crew who could get the ship into a berth while we sorted out the problem.

There was only one man on board, and he was very sick. The medics took him to the hospital and before any diagnostic work could be done, he died. An autopsy revealed a contagious tropical disease so we quarantined the ship and buried the fellow in a Chinese section of a large cemetery in Gibraltar. His personal papers told us he was a Canadian citizen from Vancouver so we forwarded all the information we had to the authorities there. After two months we had a reply telling us that the identification documents were all forgeries, and that they had no record of the man in their provincial records.

When the three-month quarantine period was over the medical people went on board to tidy up, and we discovered that there was a safe in the wall of the main cabin. There was also a well-kept logbook of all activity up until the departure from Marseilles.

The ship had started with a crew of the captain and two others but there was only the one man on board on arrival in Gibraltar. We could only assume that the two missing men had died, and were buried by the survivor who brought the ship into the bay in Gibraltar.

We had our police experts open the safe, and found the ship's owner's purchase contract, and a paid up insurance policy covering the loss of life of the captain and the loss of the ship. The beneficiary named in the policy was Patricia Quinn, and a Vancouver address was given."

No one could mistake the look of astonishment on Patricia's face. There was a long silence and then she said, "My father, in the Chinese fashion and custom, had agreed to give me in marriage to the man who was the ship's captain, but only when I finished my education. I attended the University of British Columbia in Vancouver and then, over the objections of the captain I registered in a program at the University of Marseilles.

In the Chinese custom the father's agreement constitutes a binding obligation roughly equal to a legal wedding ceremony. I did not want to marry the captain, and when my father was killed I considered the agreement null and void.

The captain apparently did not, and when the course of studies here was nearing the final two weeks he was waiting for me at the end of the class. He said they had come to take me home as soon as I was finished. Then they suddenly vanished, and I heard no more about them until this moment."

Mr. Truegood went on, "As I indicated the ship is in the Gibraltar marina. There are a number of outstanding invoices owing to the harbormaster for rental, services, the funeral costs and so on. She is a beautiful ship. One of the wealthy merchants in the city has offered two million dollars US if you should be interested in selling her. After the deductions are made there would be about 1.8 million US left as well as the five hundred thousand life insurance of the captain."

All eyes were focused on Patricia. She smiled and said, "Gentlemen, it is nearly lunch time. Let us go to the Auberge, and after lunch I will give you my decision. I would like to call the Mayor and invite him to join us for lunch."

When coffee had been served Patricia said, "Gentlemen, I have a simple announcement to make. I will accept the offer for the sale of the ship, and would like to advise the Mayor that all the proceeds of the sale will be donated to the village here for the purpose of building a school.

Second, since my family suffered serious financial loss due to the action of the ship's captain and the tong I would like to give them the life insurance policy proceeds to ensure a bit of comfort for my mother in her declining years, and to guarantee a decent education for my younger sister, and for my other sister's children."

The Mayor seemed to be unable to find any words, and after a moment Mr. Truegood said, "This is very generous of you madam. It may be, that the Harbor Master, can shade some of the charges to help support a worthy cause."

He looked at the representative, from the French Attorney General's office. He thought about the matter and then said, "I believe we have a process for forgiving taxes on the donation of such a windfall."

The three visitors thanked us for lunch and took their leave. The Mayor found his voice and thanked Patricia.

As Patricia and I walked home I remembered that night so many months ago when I had opened the safe, saw Patricia's passport and the berthing receipts, and nearly put all of the papers back in the safe. On the spur of the moment, wanting to get out and away as quickly as possible, I took the briefcase and a few receipts and locked the rest of the papers in the safe. Later that evening when we had come home and I discovered the four American million dollar certificates, and realized what I had stumbled onto and then had put them on the floor below the bottom drawer just before I was going to get into bed.

I heard a sound behind me and turned around to see

Patricia in her pajamas.

She said, "I'm cold, and frightened and lonely. May I come in?"

I said, "Yes, of course, but you don't have to do this, you know."

"I want to, very much."

I wanted her, too. I held her close for a long time before I started to unbutton her pajamas and then she said, in a very small voice,

"Please be patient with me, I've never done this before."

The anxiety of the evening slipped away, and I suddenly found myself in a whole new world that I had often wondered about, and in vague way longed for so often. And now that world had wrapped itself around me with a cloak of wonder and magic.

When I awoke in the morning she was still there with all the wonder and magic. I wanted it to be there for me always.

She seemed to take a great delight in gathering strawberries, and once more we went hunting the big dark red ones so full of juice and flavor. In the middle of this berry fest I asked her to marry me. She smiled that smile that seemed to light up the room and said, "Oh yes, I want to so much."

"Then lets get dressed and go to town to a jewelry shop, and then we can make an appointment for the mayor to do the ceremony. Perhaps you don't know that in France church ceremonies have no legal status only a civil ceremony done by a mayor or other person given special authorization. If you want we can have a church ceremony later on, and invite your family over for a holiday and a celebration."

"I would love that, but I don't think they could afford the costs. The insurance money will be slow in coming."

"Suppose we do thing as simple as send a half million dollars to your sister so they can, and then she and your mother will be taken café of for the rest of their lives."

"Can you afford to do that?"

"Yes. Will you call your sister, and get the necessary information as to where the money should be sent. Don't tell her how much is coming."

We drove back to the jewelry shop in Marseilles. The jeweler seemed surprised to see me again, especially when I asked for an engagement ring. I rejected the first tray of rings he brought out, and we finally found a square cut, four karat diamond ring and a matching wedding band.

I said, to the jeweler "She will need an elegant pair of dangling diamond ear rings and a rope of pearls."

She wanted to wear them all to make sure she wasn't dreaming, and then she looked wistfully at me and said, "Yesterday I was a waif and today I am a queen."

On the way home she kept looking at her rings as if she wanted to make sure they had not vanished how in a dream. It was after five when we arrived home, so I poured us each a drink and said, "It has been a busy day hasn't it. Would you like to go to the Auberge for dinner and meet the people? They are going to be your friends and neighbors for a long time."

It was quiet as we entered and sat down at a table for two. A moment, later Lisa came out from the kitchen and noticed me. She called to one in the kitchen "Jim is here".

In a couple of minutes Giselle, Denise and Klaus were at the table with excited hugs, kisses and "Where have you been? Comments. Then they noticed Patricia. Everyone was silent for a moment and then I took her hand, she stood up and I said, "This is my beloved, Patricia."

I introduced them and they all hugged her. Mrs. St. Onge had joined the group and when there was a moment of silence Mrs. St. Onge said, "Welcome to our family. I'm delighted you have come to take care of Jim."

Mr. St.Onge led us into the family sitting room and in a few minutes drinks were served. George and Robert joined us, and then Lisa noticed Patricia's engagement ring.

At dinner, Mr. St.Onge sat at the head of the table with Patricia at his right as the guest of honor. The wine flowed freely and everyone was having a fine time celebrating Patricia's arrival into our community.

On the way home she took my arm and said, "So that is what it is like to be adopted into a family. I'm just overwhelmed by it all," and then after a few minutes she said, "I shall never forget this evening." Then after a few moments, "Mr. St.Onge believes you are a combination of genius, magician and superman. What have you been doing?"

"Waiting for you to come along and join me."

When we arrived home it was too early to go to bed so I suggested a bit of music and a glass of wine to relax, and her response was instant

" Do you have any Mozart selections?"

"How about his ballet music?"

She seemed to just nest down and closed her eyes as the music swept over us. For a moment I thought she was asleep, but she took an occasional sip of wine and seemed to be absorbing the music into every pore in her body. Here was a new facet of her personality, and I was soon to find out more about her interest in music.

Three days later, we went to Rennes-sur-Mer, a city a dozen miles away, and poked around the shops. While we were there, we came upon an imposing music store. I wanted to look for new selections so we went in, and I was soon lost going through selections of Beethoven and Mozart.

Behind a glass wall separating the front of the store was a large room with a number of pianos, one of them a magnificent grand. I gradually became aware of one of the Chopin's nocturnes being played. Lovely I thought, and went on with what I was doing.

A few moments later I was interrupted by the store manager who said, "I used to be a concert pianist before an accident broke of my fingers. I don't know who the lady is playing that piano, but she is very talented."

I looked through the window, and saw Patricia sitting at the grand piano, seemingly lost in the Chopin music, and oblivious to all the attention she was getting.

I asked the manager, "How long would it take you to install a piano like that in my house?"

"Where do you live?"

" The St. Onge village."

"Ah, yes, we could have the piano here from Paris in seven days, and then it would take about one half day to assemble and tune it, ready for use."

" That is my fiancé at the piano, and it would be a nice birthday present for her. I will have her out of the house the day you arrive. If you check in at the Auberge St.Onge, I will have someone there with the house keys and instructions on where to place the piano."

I paid the bill, took my records, and stood behind the window waiting until Patricia finished the piece she was playing. She seemed lost in the music, and when she finished, the people in the store burst into applause. She looked around, and then smiled, and came out to where I was standing.

The store manager was not one to miss an opportunity and he said, to Patricia, "Would you consider doing a recital Sunday afternoon here in the city? We would pay you well".

She was as surprised as I was and she looked at me, obviously wanting me to comment.

" Do you have a charitable organization that might benefit from such a recital?" I asked.

"We have an orphanage and an old folks home, both of whom could use financial help."

I turned to Patricia and said, "Would you like to do this, and how much time would you need to practice for such a recital?"

"Can we find a piano in the village for me to practice on?"

"I think so."

"Then lets take the orphanage on first and start in a month. If we can get interest in the city, we can do a second one three weeks later for the old folks home."

We gave the manager our phone number and went out to find lunch.

"That was good of you to offer the help for the

orphanage." I said.

"I know what tight budgets mean. I wish I had more to give them."

"Perhaps we can find a few extra dollars by the time the recital rolls around."

I felt like a hypocrite as I thought of the four bearer bonds that were hidden in my dresser drawer. I had to figure out a way to get them to my Swiss bank, and then we could give Patricia a bank account to play around with. Perhaps we could take a few days off after the wedding ceremony and go to Strasbourg and then across to Basle, and get those bonds in a branch of my Swiss bank.

We could scatter a bit of confetti in the car, and not get much attention from the border guards and slip through customs examination.

We went home, it never occurred to me that we were approaching the threshold of a new chapter in our lives, a chapter that would reveal quite clearly the amazing talent, and the equally amazing generosity of this woman who had chosen to, as Mrs. St.Onge had so delicately phrased it, "come to take care of Jim."

CHAPTER SEVEN

The Mayor's civil ceremony was simple enough to arrange. I wondered how George was coming along with the construction of our church so that we might get Mom and Dad and Patricia's family over for a fancy church wedding and a real celebration.

We had some difficulty tracking down an organization that could make the kind of windows we wanted, but finally found a school at Chartres where they knew all about colors in glass and had some of the finest designers available. We were curious and anxious as we awaited the news of the delivery and installation.

I wondered if I could persuade Mom and Dad to retire here in the village. We could easily build a separate two bedroom stone cottage attached to our house. They could have all the privacy they wanted, and still be as much a part of the family as they wished. It was not likely that

Patricia's family would be interested in leaving all their cultural connections in Vancouver, and come to a new land with its different customs and language but we would see. They were a resilient, adaptable people.

At home I asked Patricia about her interest and studies in music.

"We had a Chinese meeting hall with an old upright piano, and I started lessons when I was five years old. It became my first love. I spent every hour I could when I was not busy with my schoolwork, and we soon discovered that I had perfect pitch, and seemed to have a gift for playing the piano. I would have enrolled in the Conservatory, if it had not been for the pressure from the tong. And then, when Dad died the whole world started cracking up, and here I am."

"Would you like to spend more time on music and the piano?"

"Mozart and Beethoven seem to be in the core of my bones and there are few things that give me greater pleasure."

I counted the days to the arrival of her piano, and then announced that I would have to go to Marseilles for shopping and would she like to go? Did she need something?

In Marseilles, I dawdled around to give the piano man all the time I could. Klaus was standing by at the Auberge to let them into the house, and to make sure the piano was set in the proper place.

When we arrived home we unpacked our purchases and then Patricia went into the living room. She stopped, looked again, gave a shriek of delight, and ran to the piano to see if it was real, struck a few keys and then came to me and said, with tears of joy running down her cheeks

"You will never know what this means to me and I will never be able to thank you enough."

I wiped away the tears, kissed her and said, "Why don't you play some of your favorite music while I make dinner?"

Next morning brought another day of glorious sunshine, and after a morning swim we were ready for breakfast.

The kitchen opened onto a small patio that butted onto the first section of the rose garden.

My experiments with roses under the pyramids had given me twenty-four bushes that I had transplanted to the garden. They were now producing the first flowers. I brought out the trolley and took all the breakfast things out to the patio. There was not a breath of wind, the sunshine was glorious and we sat there enjoying our breakfast and the flowers.

I remembered the morning, so many years ago, when Mom and I were sitting at breakfast after Dad had left for work. She told me that shortly after she and Dad were married, she enrolled in the Cordon Bleu Cooking School. It had been expensive and a great deal of hard slogging, but it had been one of the best things she had ever done.

The teachers had all come from the main school in France, and she had observed them as carefully as she could. They seemed to have one thing in common –an overtone ran through everything they did that was hard to define. They seemed to have a genius for making exactly the right sauce to give the flavor to a dish, and in indefinable way they seemed to carry this overtone throughout their daily lives.

She went on to say, "I don't know what the right word is, perhaps a combination of élan, chic, and flair combined into an invisible "sauce" that lends so much charm and delight to their lives."

That conversation left a powerful impression on my mind, and may have been one of the subconscious driving forces that brought me to France and to St.Onge.

Patricia looked carefully at the rose shrubs and then said, "We used to have roses in the garden in Vancouver, but they were nothing like the size and the depth of color you have here."

"These shrubs have all spent months growing under a pyramid. I do not know anything about the energy that pyramids produce but it does rather interesting things, as you can see by these roses. In time I would like to have a rose garden for all our corporation buildings.

You haven't had an opportunity to see the rose garden on the outside patio at the Auberge. It is delightful, and Mr. and Mrs. St.Onge are spending many happy hours out there when things are quiet at the inn. George and Giselle's house is next, but the progress is slow. I will have to increase our production line to take care of all the village needs.

There is one other thing you should know. The red and white wine, we all enjoy so much, are products from two nearby vineyards. They are very ordinary table wines, until they are placed under a pyramid and exposed to the pyramid's energy for a few weeks. Then they become super products.

At the end of the grazing field that abuts onto the hill,

hidden behind shrubs, there is a cave where we have nearly one thousand bottles getting the pyramid treatment. You will have noticed that the Auberge serves its clients with a carafe of "house wine" and serves none in a bottle with a label on it."

"I have been experimenting with calvados, cognac, champagne, and have come across a burgundy that is little short of sensational. I want to get a few hundred bottles when the next crop comes out of the vineyard. When George and Klaus taste that one they will be beating down the door."

"Can we buy a couple hundred bottles of the stuff without being conspicuous?"

"I have two hundred in the basement here in the house going through the treatment process. In a couple of weeks we will get Mr. St.Onge over here on some pretext, keep him here for lunch, and then we can get an opinion from a master."

"I expect that the manager from the Music Master shop will be on the phone shortly as he can recognize an opportunity when it comes up. Can you sketch out what might be a program to give the critics something to get excited about? You will be very much an unknown for the first recital."

"Since things are quiet in the village, would you like to spend a week or ten days in Strasbourg and Switzerland as newly wed tourist? George and Klaus will keep an eye on the place while we are gone."

"I'd love to, but we are not newly weds yet. I'm still waiting for you to make an honest woman of me"

"Of course. Lets ask Madam St.Onge if we can hold the

ceremony in the Auberge on Sunday afternoon, and then we can have a reception and celebration right there. I'm sure the Mayor will come and do the deed and then it will all be legal."

"Then we will have a reason to wander off to Strasbourg and Switzerland."

The people at the Auberge pulled out all the stops for the occasion. The short ceremony went off without a hitch, and then we had a fine rollicking celebration. Patricia and I left at five to go home to get ready for the next day's departure, but the party was still in high gear.

The drive through rural France was a delight, and when we finally arrived at Strasbourg. Patricia was fascinated by the magnificent old cathedral, and the surrounding areas; their history of being German possessions for a while, and then after another war, becoming French again. We saw the beginnings of the appearance of the new European Union.

Before we left for the Swiss border and the highway to Basle, I scattered a bit more confetti around the car. When we got to the customs post, the officer looked in the car, saw the confetti, smiled at us, and after a cursory look at our passports waved us on our way. I breathed a sigh of relief, and hoped for a quiet evening in our hotel in Basle before I ventured to the bank in the morning.

When I arrived at the bank in the morning they showed me into an account manager's office. He examined the four certificates carefully, and said they were genuine.

What would you like us to do with the money?" he asked.

"I would like three million to be added to my account and a new account opened up for my wife. She is at the hotel up the street at the moment, but I will have her come in after lunch, and you can do all the necessary work entailed in opening the account for her."

"Very good, sir, we will be expecting you."

Patricia looked puzzled when I suggested she come with me to the bank, but went along happily. They ushered us into the account manager's office. He was old world courtesy at its best to Patricia. He examined her passport with care, and then gave her bankbook with the necessary instructions for identification and withdrawal procedures.

She opened the book looked at the figure and said, "One hundred thousand dollars?"

" Madam, that is one million dollars."

She looked from him to me, shook her head, and put the book in her purse.

Later, as we were walking along the avenue, we came to a large Rolex sign in a jewelry store window and I said, "We really should have a nice souvenir of this trip to Switzerland. Why not a Rolex watch for each of us?"

"My Timex is still working very well, I really don't need a new watch." she said.

"How about a nice, decorative piece of jewelry for a beautiful lady, instead of a utilitarian Timex.?"

They had a special display of ladies' watches, the centerpiece of the display was one with diamonds placed at the hour markers on the dial, and a rim of diamonds around the whole face of the watch. I saw her eyebrows rise as she saw the price tag, and she quickly put it back.

"Is it waterproof?" I asked the sales clerk.

"Waterproof, self winding and guaranteed for the life of the original owner."

"What would it look like on your wrist?"

She undid the leather strap on her Timex and soon had the Rolex on her wrist.

"Looks great to me," I said, "We will take it. Now can we find one for me? Waterproof, no diamonds and life time guarantee please."

We went window-shopping on the other side of the bridge, and then back to the hotel in time to have a drink before dinner. They had a string quartet playing Mozart selections. We were beginning to enjoy Switzerland very much indeed.

Two days later we were in Geneva, and once again I was surprised, or was it astonished, at a new facet of Patricia's personality, not seen before. We were walking around and came upon a rather run down, untidy area that seemed to have some of the drug scene around. We did not want to appear conspicuous, so we continued to look in shop windows as we walked along to get back over the bridge and away from the area.

Patricia saw something in a clothing store window that caught her fancy, and reaching out to take my elbow with her right hand, she pointed the item out to me with her left hand. In so doing the sun was reflected off the diamonds on her watch, and caught the attention of one of the rough looking characters standing close by.

It took only a moment for him to produce a switchblade, and standing in front of Patricia he showed her the knife and said, "Give me your watch, quickly"

Before I could really comprehend what was happening, Patricia had given this thug a sharp knee in the groin, and as he was bent over with the pain he took a karate chop on the side of his neck, dropped the knife and fell unconscious on the sidewalk.

Patricia looked at the thug lying there, then took my arm and said, "He may not be interested in watches for some time,"

The few people who had observed this exchange were wide-eyed and silent as we walked away. A few moments later, Patricia said, "After the tongs moved into the Chinese community in Vancouver things got a bit rough, and father enrolled my sister and I in a martial arts course on Saturday mornings."

I smiled at her and said, "I promise to behave all the days of my life."

She laughed, "You could buy me a drink at the hotel and take me to bed to celebrate the triumph of good over evil." .

Later that evening, as we were sitting at dinner in the hotel restaurant I asked Patricia, "When you were going to high school, did you ever have any dreams about or ambitions to go to exotic places or countries?"

"In my last year in high school we had a teacher who had spent a couple of years in Egypt studying the history of the ancient dynasties and wandering around at Luxor and the upper Nile. He was a frustrated archaeologist and really mesmerized by the wonders of Sakura hieroglyphs and the Valley of the Kings."

"I think Dad is on the verge of retirement and I would like them to come out for a visit in September when some of the tourist pressure is removed. Could we arrange a four visit to see the wonder of Egypt? It's just a short flight from Marseilles to Cairo and then we might spend ten days or so in Greece as well. Mom and Dad would certainly enjoy that. I don't think they have ever been out of Canada–well to the US, of course."

The string quartet was playing again so we took out time over dinner, and then went upstairs to our room to see if there was anything worthwhile on the TV.

Tomorrow we would start on our way home, as Patricia had to get the details of the recital straightened out. She needed time to get back to a regular routine of practice.

We arrived home to find an urgent message from the manager of the Music Master shop. Two years earlier the city had made available a scholarship to the Paris Conservatory for a young local soprano. She had heard of the recital for the orphanage, and asked if she could be allowed to sing two or three songs as part of the program. She wanted to say thank you to the community for their help in her education. Could we possibly come to the shop on Sunday afternoon to discuss the whole matter?

When we arrived we found the manager waiting with a very attractive young lady. She was very apologetic about intruding in the program, but she couldn't manage a whole afternoon of her own.

"Its probably heaven sent opportunity for both of us." Patricia said, "What songs would you like to sing?"

" One Fine Day' from Madame Butterfly, the 'Jewel Song ' from Faust, and the 'Barcarolle" from Tales of Hoffman."

"Do you have an accompanist?" Patricia asked.

"No, I was hoping you might help me."

"Of course. Exactly as the composer wrote it?"

"Yes."

We listened in the demonstration room, and were astonished at the power and clarity of her voice and even more so when she sang the Barcarolle. The range through that she traveled with such ease and grace was surprising. Here was a voice destined for the operatic stage in the future.

When they had tidied up the details Patricia said, "I'm told there is a Veterans' home here in the city that might welcome a benefit concert later in the year. Could we manage that as well?"

There was a long silence and then the young lady said, "My father lives in that Veterans' home. I would be so happy to be a part of that concert."

It was Patricia's turn to pause for a moment and then she said, "Will you please help me with the selection of the music for the program as this will be a whole new world to me?"

"Of course, I grew up with many of these are songs, soldier's songs and ballads out of the classical repertoire. I will get the music and forward a proposal on to you as soon as possible. I'm so grateful to you for doing this."

" Could you come to lunch with us now?" I asked her.

We found a restaurant, and when we were settled over our drinks waiting for the mussels to appear, I tried to get a bit of background information on this young lady–Francine Couperand by name. She was having a difficult struggle keeping herself in the Conservatory in Paris. I was astonished, and asked her if we could give her a bit of help.

Unless I was very much mistaken this voice would be a sensation for many years to come and any small assistance we could give her would be returned to society to an unimaginable degree. Would she like a private voice teacher? Oh yes, but they were so expensive. Did she known one? Ah, yes.

When we had finished our lunch, the three of us went to the bank, and we opened up a bank account in her name, She promised to arrange for a voice teacher as soon as she was back in Paris. She was wide eyed with disbelief that she would have all the money she could use.

"There is one other thing." I said, "Where are your traveling things at this moment?"

"A small suitcase is in the Music Master's shop. I don't have many things."

"From this moment on, your home is our home and our home is your home. You will be a part of our family. Can you come with us now? Patricia will take you through the department store to get you the things you need, and we will all go back to the village where you will meet the other members of your St.Onge family."

Two and a half hours later the three of us carried all her boxes and parcels to her room in Warburton House, and we told her that this was her home for the rest of her life. She looked around, and Patricia saw the tears of gratitude coming and then said, "There is time for a swim before we go to the Auberge for dinner. Last one in the pool is a monkey."

After the hard days in the orphanage and at school" Francine said, to me, " I must have died and gone to Heaven. How will I ever be able to repay you?"

"Repay? Repay? Just love everyone in the village and be part of our family."

The first of the new crop of wines was starting to appear on the market, and I carefully scouted around the region. I was busy so Patricia had uninterrupted days to practice, and I was delighted to see how happy and contented she was at the end of each day.

A week later she said, "Could we have our corporation friends over on Sunday next for a pool party? I could have a mini-concert to show off my new piano."

At the party, we swam and played and then had lunch. I noticed Mr. St.Onge sipping his wine and looking at me from time to time. After lunch he refilled his glass, and we listened to Patricia play some of her favorite pieces, and then we went back to the pool.

Mr. St.Onge came to me lifted his wine glass and said, "This is new and is superb. Have you been holding out on us?"

"No, not at all. It comes from a vineyard north of Marseilles, where the soil seems to be quite different. I found two-dozen bottles in a wine shop, and put them under the pyramid. I tried the first one a few days ago, and my reaction is like yours. This was part of last year's crop and I have ordered three hundred bottles for delivery in a few weeks."

He called Klaus over and asked him for his opinion

"I was going to ask where it came from and if there was any more of it for me to take home. It is very good indeed."

"The vineyard is about twenty miles west of here along the river bank. The soil seems to be different. I've three hundred bottles on order from this year's crop. I don't want to get the owner excited by ordering a large quantity, as he might want to raise the price. Would you go over and lay in an order for another three hundred as this won't last long in the Auberge and the corporation."

Mr. St.Onge said, "The Auberge is doing quite nicely with the existing stocks, let's keep this within the corporation until we run down our present inventory."

"We obviously cannot send the Auberge van with its' sign painted on the doors over to the vineyard, but if Robert were to take the Charboneau, Leitman Construction van over, it would not arouse their curiosity, and so get him to raise the price of the wine. He will deliver three hundred bottles here, that should not cause any comment, but we don't know what his total output is or what his regular clientele list looks like.

"Can the Auberge basement storage hold three hundred bottles in process while using up the present inventory?"

"No, we don't have that much space available."

"Then it can go into the cave without any trouble, and we can distribute as needed to the corporation members."

Two weeks later we were on our way to do the first benefit concert at Rennes-sur-Mer. The Music Master had done his advertising work well, so there were not many vacant seats in the hall.

After a short announcement and introductions by the Music Master, Patricia played twenty minutes of Chopin nocturnes, and then bowed her thanks to their enthusiastic applause.

Francine, the soprano, then came out and did her first number.

The crowd rose to give her a standing ovation. It was the same for the rest of the concert. When they were finished the crowds kept calling for an encore. The girls had something ready, and then finally Patricia had to play the national anthem to get them to break up and go home.

As we were about to leave Patricia produced an envelope and gave it to the Music Master and said, "Will you please add this to the day's receipts for the donation to the orphanage?"

He opened the envelope, looking puzzled and then opened his mouth as if wanting to say thing, but nothing came out. He looked at Patricia like a fish out of water. He finally managed a thank you as we said, goodbye.

As we were driving home she was smiling with a grin like a Cheshire Cat and then said, "The cheque was for fifty thousand American dollars."

"Could you have found a more deserving group of beneficiaries?"

"If we get the same kind of enthusiastic crowd at the next concert it will be the making of a reputation for Francine."

"We can manage another fifty thousand dollars for them. Let us sit on our hands until we get the response of the critics to this first concert. That voice deserves the best teacher there is. Perhaps we could help a bit. Can you sound her out when next you are chatting? Or better still, when she is here for a weekend, see what is on her horizon. That is a most unusual talent and should be trained and nurtured. "

After dinner that evening, I suggested that it was now time to give attention to the culling of the first crop of two-year old Black Angus cattle.

The phone rang, and when Patricia answered it we

were enchanted to hear Francine tell us that she had just been advised that Covent Garden wanted her to come and sing Tosca in the spring, and that she was going to make her operatic debut singing Norma for the opening of the winter season in Berlin. Would we like to come?

"Can't wait!"

After we hung up the phone I said, to Patricia, "I will go to see the doctor who services the Veteran's Home tomorrow, and see if it is possible to get permission for Francine's father to join us for the trip to Berlin to see the performance. What a lovely surprise that would be for Francine! There is a straight train run from Marseilles to Berlin, and we can take care of him on the trip. He will never have been on one of the high speed trains, and will enjoy the trip."

CHAPTER EIGHT

Black Angus cattle were surprisingly difficult to find in the beef markets in that southern sector of France. Our search finally took us to Luxemburg where we found a number of purebred herds from which we could make a choice for our gene pool. Patricia had done a good deal of research into optimum nutrition grazing crops for these animals, and we were now about to have our first experience with the beef market.

The port being so close and the North Africa competitors being so active, the market was only going to reward beef producers who had an excellent product at a most competitive price.

Patricia had been curious about what the Auberge people had been doing about their meat supplies.

Mr. St.Onge said,. "Now that our kitchen and cold storage facilities have been greatly increased, we are able to reduce the many hours we used to spend each week going to the market to purchase produce and meat. We have been dealing with a small private slaughterhouse in Rennes-sur-Mer. If you are ready to cull your cattle, let us get the fellow out here to have a look at them and see what, if anything, can be arranged for the benefit of all of us."

When the fellow appeared a few days later, he walked around through the herd, made notes, and then said, "At a rough first guess, I'd say this is one of the best herds I have ever seen. What we don't know is the amount of fat per pound. We would have to slaughter one to see what this range-fed nutrition program of yours is giving in the final product. Then we can determine a fair price for the various cuts."

They chose one of the two-year-old bulls, and took him off to the slaughterhouse. Four days later, they were back with a box of well cut and vacuum wrapped samples of roasts, fillets and hamburger.

"We have left samples at the Auberge as well. You will have noticed that we chose the largest fattest young bull we could find in the herd. We were astounded to find that the fat on the animal was the smallest percentage we have ever seen on any animal coming into the slaughterhouse. We are ask that you and the people at the Auberge use the meat in your recipes to see what we are getting for tenderness and flavor."

"The best test I can imagine is to have one of the fillet mignon steaks for our dinner this evening, and then we can talk to the people at the Auberge about their taste testing activities."

When I came home at five Patricia met me at the door

with a couple of honest gin drinks in hand, gave me one and said, "A toast to greener pastures for departed Black Angus two year olds."

"May they all be green and luscious"

So we sat in the kitchen feasting on our broiled steaks and mushrooms. I was watching Patricia for a reaction as she tried the meat. After a while she said, "You can almost cut the meat with a fork, and I have never known such flavor."

Then she went on, "I wonder what they have done at the Auberge by way of trying the samples?"

We didn't have to wait long to find out. We had scarcely cleaned away the dishes before the doorbell rang.

To our surprise it was Mr. and Mrs. St.Onge.

Patricia offered coffee, and we could see they were excited about something.

Then Mr. St Onge said, "I believe the butcher fellow brought you meat samples today?"

"Yes, and we had two of the fillet mignon steaks for dinner this evening."

Both of the St.Onge's were waiting for a further comment and finally Patricia said, "I could almost cut it with my fork and I have never before found such flavor."

Madam St. Onge said, "We invited the whole family over, prepared a large roast and fillets and then shared with everybody. Our reaction was the same."

There was a long silence as they drank their coffee, and then I said, "Do you know who owns the property joining onto ours here on the west side?"

It took a moment for the significance of the question to sink in, and then Mr. St.Onge said, "Of course, it is a gold mine waiting to be discovered. I think the Mayor owns it."

"Could the Corporation buy it at a reasonable price?"

"I know him well enough to call him at home. I'll find out the size as well."

He went to the phone and made his call while we chatted about the beef, and then came back and said, "He has been paying taxes on it for years, and it has produced no revenue. He would be pleased to sell all 150 hectares for fifty thousand American dollars."

"Can you call him back and tell him we will be happy to buy it from him for seventy five thousand American dollars. We will close the deal tomorrow."

"But," he said.

"I know, but we have to be fair to him. We will have to live with him for a long time."

Madame St. Onge looked at me and said, "You mentioned a cheese that I do not know–Stilton?"

"It is an English cheese that seems to fit my mouth very well. I had to smuggle some into the country, as I did not want to have to face a firing squad for bringing a cheese into a country that has as many wonderful cheeses as France does."

I went on, "We are having Francine, the soprano, as a house guest for the weekend. She and Patricia are going to iron out the program for a recital in Rennes-sur-Mer next month. May I invite you to join us for dinner on Friday and then we will sample the delights of music and song and Stilton cheese."

"We would be enchanted."

Next morning I laid out the events for Patricia; the Mayor to sign off the deed, a fencing contractor, Patricia's formula for recovery of the land and its grazing for a new herd, contact with our first time suppliers of cattle in Luxemburg, and discussion with Klaus over the design of a water supply for the new grazing land.

When I paused Patricia laughed and said, "How long will it take Mr. St. Onge to raise the issue of an addition to the Auberge?"

"Three years, is my guess."

We picked Francine at the Marseilles airport at noon on Friday and as soon as we were home everyone headed for the pool.

We told Francine that Mr. and Mrs. Sy.Onge were coming to dinner. What we had not told her was that they had arranged to bring her father to the Auberge for the weekend and they were going to bring him.

So at five we left the pool to get ready for dinner. Patricia and I were busy in the kitchen with Francine.
When the doorbell rang. Patricia said, "Francine would you be a dear and let them in, please?"

We followed a moment later, just in time to see the look of happiness on Francine's face as her father came in.

Introductions made, we sat down to enjoy our drinks and get acquainted.

Patricia gathered us around the dinner table after a while. The shrimp disappeared quickly, and then out came the trolley with the fillet mignon and potato mystery for our new experience for the St.Onge experts.

They looked carefully, we explained how it was done and then they took their first taste of the meat and the potato.

Mr. St. Onge rolled the food around in his mouth and

then said, pointing to me, "This man has so many secrets we will have to get him on the rack to extract them. This is marvelous."

Then Patricia sprang her strawberry-ice cream and calvados surprise on them.

Mr. St. Onge looked at his wife and said, "If we put this on the menu, we would have to double our seating capacity in two years."

We enjoyed our coffee and brandy, and then the girls cleaned up while I found a movie they would all enjoy.

Then it was time for them to go back to the Auberge, so we said, good night and promised to come over to the Auberge for lunch the next day so Francine could meet the rest of the family and spend time alone with her father.

As we left Madam St.Onge said, to Patricia and I, "The whole family will be there for dinner, please come."

What we thought was going to be a quiet Saturday evening turned out rather differently.

The Auberge was filled with tourists and local folk out for dinner, and then I was rash enough to suggest that Patricia and Francine do a few numbers to entertain the visitors.

Two hours later the place was still full of people ordering more rounds of drinks and shouting for encores. Finally the girls played the national anthem, and then disappeared into the kitchen.

I waited until the crowd cleared to help.

Mr. St.Onge said, "We have never taken in so much money in one evening before."

Next morning the three of us went to the Auberge to see if Francine's father would like to go to the church service with us.

"He discovered the church yesterday, fell in love with it, and is there now." Mrs. St Onge told us.

As we sat in the church we noticed people going up to the priest who was to conduct the service. They pointed to us in the third row, and after a few moments the priest came to Francine and asked her if she would sing the opening hymn, Schubert's "Ave Maria", and then a second one of her choice for the closing.

After the service we made our way back to the Auberge. Denise brought us wine and Patricia said, to Francine, "You seemed to be so happy singing in the church."

"Like you, I feel adopted, they all seem like members of my family. They really are my people. No matter where I have gone or will ever go this part of the country will always be my home. I would like to make it even more so."

Madame St.Onge had prepared a feast of mussels, and we all rolled up our sleeves. From the attention she paid Francine's father I suspect it was his favorite dish.

All too soon it was time for Francine to go to the airport in Marseilles and back to Paris, and for her father to go home to Rennes-sur-Mer.

Later as the three of us made our way to Marseilles Patricica said, to Francine, "Your father seems like such a nice, warm, gentle, loving man."

There was a pause, and then Francine said, "I can never recall him raising his voice. It was always soft, gentle and loving. He worked hard for a construction company, all his working life, and he and I spent whatever time we could together going places and seeing things."

"Your mother?"

There was a long pause and then Francine said, "She spent all her married life flying around on her broom and screaming…I spent as much time as I could in my room on my studies to avoid her. Dinnertime was always an agony, and I determined at an early age that I would never get involved in a loveless marriage. When she died a few years ago, going to her funeral was one of the hardest things I ever had to do. I know the next one will be even more so but for the opposite reason."

There was silence until we arrived at the airport a few minutes later, and then, to my surprise, an astonishing display of emotion between these two. Love, hugs, tears and then Francine turned to me and said, "I have not seen so much love among people as I have this week-end. May I come back another time to be with you?"

"We would love to have you anytime and as often as you can get away. I need you to help me convert Patricia and make her a true devotee of the love of garlic loaded snails."

"Soon, soon, we will redeem her from the heathen hordes." She laughed took her small suitcase and disappeared in the direction of the aircraft.

We made our way along the main highway home, and then Patricia dropped the bombshell.

She had long intimate conversations with Francine and Francine told her that she was very sensitive to the environment around her after living in such a barren loveless home as her mother had created.

She wanted to have two or three children, but she would never marry a man she did not love and the man she loved was already married.

Then Patricia told me that recently she and Denise had been to Rennes-sur-Mer to see a gynecologist, who told her she wouldn't be able to conceive. Patricia wanted children and knew that I did as well. She had been trying to get pregnant without success. She mentioned this to Francine.

It was then that Francine told her that IF Patricia was open to the offer, Francine would be very happy to volunteer to become a surrogate mother for a child or two or three for us. Since she was a large woman no one would notice her being pregnant until her fifth month and then she would take the next five months off from her operatic schedule and go to Greece. She would have the baby and them we could go to Greece on a holiday, and come home with an adopted baby. She would know that her child was growing up in the best possible circumstances, and she could see the child as time permitted. The benefits for all were obvious.

Patricia continued, "She wants children and she wants them to grow up in this part of France, she will have plenty of money to take care of their education and future, but she does want them to absorb the environment of this area.

I drove along for a while, turning the whole matter over in my mind, then said, "It is a bit strange, but it does have merit, I suppose. Are you convinced that the gynecologist is right? How about a second opinion?"

"This was a second opinion."

"This certainly gets complicated, but Francine seems to have thought about this whole matter at length. Did she tell you who is the man she is in love with, and wants as the father of her children?"

"You."

I was so startled I nearly missed the turn off of the main highway. It took me a long time to recover, and then I said, "I have the best wife in the world, and I will have to talk about this to her when I get home."

As usual, Patricia was miles ahead of me, so when we arrived home she said, "By the way, it is time to check the swimming pool filters. Why don't you do that while I get dinner ready?"
It took her only a few minutes to get a couple of honest drinks ready and prepare the steaks.

Later we sat over our coffee she opened the conversation again, saying, "I have done everything possible based on the best advice I could get from three different and highly respected gynecologists, to get pregnant. The problem clearly lies with me and it seems I will never be able to have a child of my own. I believe you want a child or children as much as I do."

Patricia continued, "I was surprised to hear, so candidly, from Francine about her growing up days in Rennes. She could not have been more determined to not get involved in a loveless marriage and repeat her father's lonely life, but she did want too have a child or two, and she did want them to grow up in an environment where they would be wanted and loved and given every opportunity for a good education and a good life, and she did want to have them with the man she had fallen in love with–if it was possible."

Patricia paused to look at me before she kept on, "For her, and for me all the pieces of the puzzle fell into place. There are millions of Muslim men who have two or more wives who are as close as sisters and live in harmony.

She is prepared to do everything possible. All she asks is that she be welcome to visit from time to time. She will go to Greece in her fifth month, on illness pretext, and then we can join her later and go through the adoption process.

Your co-operation in what should be a not too painful process is all that is required to set the whole drama in motion. You would be bringing a great deal of happiness into the lives of at least five people."

"Five?"

"Yes, I'm sure that when your parents have a grandchild or two to spoil. They will be more pleased than you can imagine."

"I'm defeated by the simplicity and the logic of the situation. I presume you have chosen a date to set the whole drama in motion?"

"Her cycles are as regular as clockwork, and she will be ready when she is here for the recital for the fundraising for the old folks home."

I looked at Patricia for a long moment, and for the first time I saw a new facet of the personality. All of this was being done, primarily, for me. I went over to her, took her in my arms and said, "And this is my beloved."

On bright sunny mornings we were usually out of bed and doing our ten laps in the pool before breakfast. Since we were the only two people in the house we didn't need swim suits. We would dry ourselves and get food, usually starting with a strawberry hunt.

Patricia was a beautiful woman, small in size, as many Chinese women are, so it was a never-ending pleasure to see her checking the strawberry plants for the best, ripest ones. It was a fun part of our lives and was brought to an end when the construction began on Francine's house. It was attached to our house with a doorway for her to enter the pool whenever she wished.

Patricia and I had a number of discussions about this arrangement. Patricia laughed as she said, "No Chinese woman would ever destroy a good working marriage because her husband had had five minutes of pleasure with another woman. In fact, most Chinese women I have known would arrange such a liaison for their husbands recognizing that they were getting older and their husband would appreciate a trip back down memory lane.

The western world with its emphasis on sex, has gotten out of focus in human relationships. If you were to give me, and us, two or three children via a surrogate mother, it would do no damage to our marriage but would build something wonderful in our lives and in Francine's life.

CHAPTER NINE

Kyros Agamemnon Popadopolis arrived in mid-morning on a bright sunny day in mid June. His arrival was noted in the local village records by the village doctor, as the law required. He also noted, that the child was being adopted by a pair of visiting foreigners. Thus there would be no ambiguity in the village records when the next census was done.

Two weeks later James and Patricia arrived back home with their newly adopted baby. He was brought to the village church and baptised as Arthur James Warburton. All the people were there to admire this beautiful, happy young addition to the village.

The adoption certificate, printed in the Greek, was incomprehensible to the guests, but had enough stamps, and seals on it to be impressive, and the adoption was noted on the parents passports at the Canadian Embassy in Paris.

One month later James and Hazel Warburton arrived, from Canada, at the airport in Marseilles for an extended visit.

When they arrived at the St.Onge village they were delighted to see the old stone house, now with a splendid growth of ivy to offset the rose garden.

They dropped their luggage in the guest room and then tiptoed into the baby's room to get a first glimpse of the grandchild.

"What a beautiful baby."

They looked around the house and pool, had coffee and cakes until it was time to feed the baby.

Jim said, to his father, "The village folk have decided to adopt you and Mom into the village family, and are planning a reception tomorrow afternoon at the Auberge to formally welcome you. They have certainly adopted Patricia and I.

You will remember the Leitman boys. Klaus was my buddy during the high school days. Klaus and his brother Robert have married two of the local girls and are obviously going to spend the rest of their lives here.

We now plow two hundred and eighty hectares of land, and a special range-feeding program designed by Patricia for our sixty-five Black Angus beef cattle. You will see of the results later."

A reception was held at the Auberge and it would be long remembered by all the villagers, but even more so by the visitors.

The local newspaper in Rennes-sur-Mer, in their social column, reported that the Mayor of Rennes-sur-Mer had attended the celebrations, but the reporter did not take note that among the honored guests at the proceedings there was one member from the Rennes-su-Mer's old folks home named Jacques Couperand, the father of the well known operatic star.

Three weeks later everyone in the village was saddened to hear the news that Mr. Couperand had passed away.

He was to be buried in the cemetery at St.Onge village after the church service. The few reporters who had been able to track down his daughter, the well known opera star, Francine Couperand, had been unable to find her, and after the ceremony had decided to go back to the city.

The architect had long since finished the reflecting pool and the rose garden around it with the terraced seats for the audience around the pool, and extended the Auberge patio seating. At the western end of the reflecting pool, George had built an elegant stone band shell.

When the graveside ceremony was over, all the people gathered at the pool seats, and the Auberge patio. The Mayor announced that there would be a few words to honor and celebrate the life of this good and decent man.

The staff of the Auberge served refreshments for the crowd, the Mayor made a speech, and Francine sang a few of her father's favorite songs.

Francine stayed with us for a few days after the funeral, and the ladies had a fine time taking turns feeding the baby. Francine then made her way to the Royal Albert Hall in London for a recital.

Jim told his parents about the recitals the two ladies had done in Rennes-sur-Mer, how they had met and become such good friends, closer than most sisters.

When mid-August rolled around the Warburtons spoke of returning to Canada. Patricia immediately raised the issue of their return to St Onge to spend their retirement. They looked surprised and then Jim said, "We already have the plans for building a two bedroom attached annex to this house. You can have as much privacy as you like, and be as much a part of the family as you wish. We have only to press the switch and get the contractor in motion. There are no cold winters here, and we would be very, very happy if you came."

Jim's father said, "I have been thinking about this. I'm tired of winter and would welcome the offer. I can retire any time I wish and there is nothing but a few friends to hold us back home. We would both enjoy life here more than life in Brampton for our retirement years."

"Your new home will be tied to this building, and will be waiting for you whenever you are ready for an old stone rose garden and a happy family."

"What about Patricia's family?"

" My mother would never be comfortable away from her Chinese friends in the church there. She would never be able to accommodate to the language and cultural differences. My sister is the principal of a school and her two children are established in their educational programs. They would not want to be uprooted, but they will come for a visit next summer."

My parents said, their good-byes to young Arthur, and I took them to the airport. On the way home I sorted out my priorities for the building of their new home here in the village. The stone was readily available, but I had better start with the new crop of roses for their garden as soon as I could so they would be ready for transplanting as soon as possible. They were Mom's favorite and she had been so delighted to see them around the village.

George was happy to sit down with Patricia and I, and work through the details of the annex. The landscaping would follow when the house was finished.

Two weeks later, Patricia and I were standing in front of the house when an expensive sports car with dark tinted windows pulled up and turned into the carport. We were delighted to see Francine get out of the car and come around the corner with her small suitcase. She had just come from Paris, and had a week of free time before she had to get on her way to Bonn for rehearsals for the opening of the opera season. She was going to sing the role of Mimi in La Boheme.

Patricia hugged her, and said, "I'm so glad you have come."

I knew the real reason for the visit, and decided to be as compliant as I could be, not that it was going to be unpleasant for Francine was a very attractive woman. The whole drama had already been set in motion and act two was about to begin. I was just given a small part in the play.

After an afternoon at the pool, Patricia and I set the scene for the most elaborate candlelight and silver dinner we could manage. After all it was going to be another red-letter day in all of our lives. Francine was delighted to be able to feed and play with the baby until he fell asleep in her arms.

We dawdled over our steaks and dessert, and then watched a movie until it was time to go to bed. It was a very quiet weekend. No one in the village came by and then, on Monday morning Francine left for Bonn as quietly as she had arrived. The curtain had fallen on act two of our drama.

Three weeks later Patricia received a phone call from her sister with the bad news that her mother had passed away. She been volunteering at the local hospital and had caught a virus. She was gone in four days. It was so sudden that no one suspected she was ill until she was admitted to the hospital, and she died the next day.

It seemed to me that nothing could be more fitting in this situation than to donate money for the hospital's reflecting pool and garden area. The money we had in the bank had originally come from the many people of the Chinese community.

The tong had raised this money through their nefarious ways. In turn Patricia's mother had lost her husband, and much of the livelihood she and her children had earned over so many years. If some of the money could be used to honor her many years of volunteering in the community the tong had treated so harshly, it might be fitting indeed.

Of course, the local folk would have to be told part of the story.

We were not surprised when a notice announcing the opening of the operatic season in Bonn arrived with twin tickets.

Patricia said, "How nice, but I am not going to leave the baby in the hands of anyone else while we go gallivanting around Europe. Do you suppose that Klaus and Lisa would like to have a holiday?"

"They certainly deserve one. Suppose we get them over

for dinner on Friday and lay the idea on them. In any case, George is going to start building the annex, and I would like to be close at hand to make sure that it's all properly laid out."

"By the way, I watched Mom in the rose garden to see if I could determine where her preferences lay as to colors in the roses. I couldn't tell. She seemed to enjoy the rose garden here when they first arrived, and the roses around the reflecting pool and the Auberge patio seemed to take her breath away. When we came away from their first viewing of the inside of then Church I heard her say, to your father, "Jim seems to have had his fingers in a lot of things in this village.""

Two weeks later, I came home from a corporation meeting to find all the candles and silver laid out as she did on most special days. She handed me a drink and said, "Once more we are going to celebrate James Arthur Warburton. Four years ago I was a frightened, poor waif wondering how I was going to escape from the thugs who had come from Vancouver to kidnap me and force me into a life of shameful servitude, threatening to do terrible things to my family if I did not co-operate. And look at me now. Surely no fairy tale could ever be more wonderful than this story."

I looked at her and said, "I would be delighted to drink a toast to the two way street we have been living on as long as I have known you. When I was in my early teens my Dad brought home a small poodle. He and I bonded instantly and he taught me one very important thing. All he had to give was a great deal of love and he was loved and cared for in return. He used to go around pushing things with his nose, and usually hit them, so we called him Gunner. He understood an age-old principle ' That in the giving is the getting'. He had his bed at the foot of my bed and was always as good as he could be. One night he jumped on my bed and without making a sound, woke me up and led me off to the front door of the house in the dark. When we got to the front door we heard noise. Someone was tampering with the lock. Gunner started barking and growling. I turned on the light and saw the two would-be burglars racing off across the lawn. Duty done Gunner waggled his tail, went back to his bed, and went to sleep."

We finished our drinks, and then sat down to feast our way through the shrimp, fillet mignon and ice cream, and then Patricia handed me a card that repeated a message I had seen once before. It said, everything in a few words..."YES, 15 July," and gave an address in Skellingsfjord, Norway.

The note was as simple as it could be, but told us everything.

That part of the world did not have a great inflow of tourists at that time of the year, so we would be renting a car in Oslo and driving to the upper end of the country.

There seems to be a shortage of male names in the Warburton line. Do you think, Thor Anderssen could become Thomas Andrew Warburton?

And now that Patricia Warburton has been through the initial pain and suffering of motherhood a first time, should we learn to count to three?

"We can leave empty trails scattered around the continent, but we will not be able to escape the sharp eyes of our friends and acquaintances here in the village. The

Warburton eyes are distinctive. Whatever they may or may not be Mr.St.Onge and her daughters are not fools."

"Well perhaps a few dollars might turn Francine into Bjarnesdottir whose husband was killed in a landslide"

After a moment's thought Patricia said, "I would be very happy with three or four but that decision should not be mine to make. Shall we give Francine the responsibility for the decision?"

"Yes. If and when she raises the issue we can pick up the ball and run with it."

We saw the glowing reports of her debut performance at the New York Metropolitan Opera in the Paris newspapers. It also said, she was to appear in Das Rhinegold in Berlin in September.

I came home in late afternoon in mid August to find her car in the carport and a strange silence in the house when I came into the living room.

I quietly made my way up the stairs and then heard a small child's laughter coming from the boy's room. Opening the door very quietly, I saw the three of them lying on the floor with their heads together playing a game not known to me, but it made the baby laugh.

Francine had ten days to rest and relax before she had to report in for the rehearsals for her next performance in Berlin. She had brought the score with her.

Looking at this beautiful woman I wondered where and when the operatic world would find a more perfect Rhine maiden.

Next morning we went to visit her father's grave. The roses we had planted along the pathway and by the grave grew profusely. We now had a simple but very impressive headstone in place. She was astonished to see the fresh flowers on the headstone. She stood by the gravesite, wiped away the tears and said, "This is the only place in France I have, to come home to. But who brought the flowers?"

"I'm sure it was the people at the Auberge," I said, "they were very fond of him you know."

We went to the Auberge. Madame St.Onge spotted us coming in, went to the kitchen door, spoke to someone and then came out to greet us, and seat us while the rest of the family came in.

Madam took the baby and said, "Grandmothers know what to do with babies," and disappeared.

The welcome could not have been warmer for Francine.

After lunch, Mr. St.Onge surprised us all by saying, "We have all been reading the critics reports on your performances in the various cities from time to time. Would you two girls do a Sunday afternoon concert for the villagers here?"

Francine and Patricia looked at each other and the both said, "Gladly."

"Good, we will make sure that all the village people know, and the Auberge will provide refreshments."

"It will have to be an unrehearsed free-for-all fun afternoon."

"And I will baby sit." It was a firm and final decision from Madam St.Onge.

We invited the manager of the Music Master shop in Rennes-sur-Mer and his family down for the afternoon. The people sitting in the Auberge patio and the terraced seats around the pool were served frees drinks and food.

When we arrived back home about six, after what must

have been an exhausting afternoon for the girls, I suggested that Mr. And Mrs. St.Onge and Klaus and Lisa might enjoy a couple of weeks of holiday in Germany, particularly Berlin. It was an easy flight from Marseilles to Berlin and they could rent a car and enjoy themselves for a couple of weeks as well as taking in the opera."

"I'll have a box reserved for them." Francine added.

CHAPTER TEN

I was watching the expression on Patricia's face when she took the phone call from Grandmother Warburton telling us they had sold their place and were coming to stay.

Mom and Dad were going to be surprised at the appearance of their second grandchild so the place ought to be a riot of sound and color until a new routine was established, but that was only peripheral for Dad and I, the ladies would be in tight control there.

I would spend time with Dad, getting him fully immersed in the farm, and in the corporation's activities. There was also one real surprise bonus for both him and I.

He had always been a great sports fisherman and now he was to get started on a new chapter of that sport. There were areas not very far away that we could get to in an hour or so and then he would have real fishing fun.

We were going to have to hurry for we did not know anything about Francine's schedule, or the facilities at Skellingsfjord. We needn't have worried. Our rental car was ready for us, and we were on the road in an hour after arriving. Traveling was more cumbersome than it used to be before Arthur arrived, but Patricia had matters well in hand.

When we arrived at the tiny village at the end of the fjord, we had only a few moments to look around before someone in a uniform asked if they might help us.

They could and did, and the clinic was easy to find. They showed us into Francine's room, and after a while, they brought in the baby. We had assumed it was going to be another boy, and we were surprised to find a beautiful red haired girl.

Patricia took one long look at her and then said, "She is the most beautiful baby girl I have ever seen."

They had arranged for us to stay at a bed &breakfast close by so we went over to get settled. Patricia was doing double duty having to find the items we would need for the new baby to travel.

With a good deal of help from the people at the B&B we got the things we needed. Then there was a tearful farewell to Francine, and we set off on the road to Oslo and home, home and a new chapter in the Warburton family's life.

I called Klaus from Orly airport in Paris to see if he could pick us up at Marseilles. I will leave his look of surprise to the reader's imagination as he saw us coming from the flight with two babies.

He looked at the baby and said, "She is a beautiful baby. Do they have them in department stores up there? I know where Lisa and I are going on our next holiday. She will see this one and want at least six."

"I'm not sure they are available on the shelf." Patricia said, "But you might try asking. Jim was clever in feeding the storks who were nesting in the chimney of the B&B we were staying at, and then when we woke up in the morning there it was."

"Does she have a name to go with that Viking head full of red hair?"

"Twyla Freya."

Klaus dropped us, the babies, the luggage, and we went into the house to try to get some organization into our lives.

Patricia said, "Both babies are sleeping, and I think that both of us need an honest drink to celebrate the successful arrival home."

"No argument."

She poured two respectable drinks, and I raised my glass and said, "Patricia, you are truly a jewel without price in the worlds of women, I love you, I honor you and am grateful for all the things you have done for me, for us and for the family."

The doorbell rang, and in marched Papa and Mama St.Onge, Klaus and Lisa, George and Giselle, Robert and Denise.

"The new baby, the new baby...." the ladies were all excited. So while I poured drinks for them, Patricia brought the baby down for all to see.

Papa St.Onge took a long look at the baby and then said, "There hasn't been a red haired Viking baby in southern France since the Viking invasion of 973." and then he took Patricia and me by the hand and said, "Please come with me for a moment."

He motioned to Klaus, and the three of us stepped into

the other room. Papa St.Onge said, "Let's go back." and there in the middle of the room were Mom and Dad. It seems there had been confusion in their routing and they had arrived two days earlier, surprised to find Patricia and I not at home. Klaus had introduced them to their new home and then prepared the surprise for them and us.

Mom greeted us and then picked up the baby. She looked at her for a long time, and then tears in her eyes, said to Patricia, "This is the most beautiful baby girl I have ever seen."

Mama St.Onge, ever the practical one, said, "You have just arrived without a stick of furniture for a new baby. We can get things from the girls until you can get to town and buy the things you need. When we finish our drinks we will go to the Auberge, and all have dinner and then the men can bring the things over."

I saw Dad standing off to one side looking in amazement at what was going on, so I went over and said, "I see you are amazed at being adopted into the family here."

"From the moment we arrived, they just gathered around us and made us feel as if we had been here all our lives."

Then, in a voice I remembered too well from my boyhood days, Mom picked up Twyla and said, to Patricia, "May I carry Twyla while you bring young Arthur?"

We made our way to the Auberge where I learned that no child can possibly have too many aunts, uncles, grandmothers and grandfathers.

Mom and Dad were soon enmeshed in the group as if they had been resident in the village for many years.

It was then that Papa St.Onge dropped the idea of getting a group of fishermen out of the village and having an annual challenge.

Papa Warburton, whose prowess as a fly fisherman was unknown here, smiled at the prospect until he heard Papa St.Onge say, "No fish under 100 kilos will be considered as eligible for the challenge. Anything that small would be used for the 'Fisherman's Dinner'."

Dad and I made ourselves as useful as possible for the next few days, trying to get the baby settled, and doing all the shopping necessary. It was a good opportunity for Dad to get to know Rennes-sur-Mer. Then the two of us went scouting the region to see if we could find a motor boat that would suit our needs, room for six men to move around, one to drive and three to fish.

We set out early on the first bright, sunny Saturday morning; Papa St.Onge, Papa Warburton, as he was now known to all, Klaus and I. For me, as the motorboat captain, it was a new and uncharted experience. Papa St.Onge had assured us that we would have to use a shiny flasher spoon at thirty meters or more as we slowly trolled out in the deep waters.

In two hours of trolling we managed to get two sixty pounders and then there was no more action.

Dad said, "I wonder if we might get more attention if I wrapped my spoon with part of the entrails of one of the fish?"

"Good idea," said, Papa St. Onge.

I stopped the boat while they reeled in, and I quickly slit up the belly of one of the fish. Each of them took about three feet, wrapped it tied tightly just ahead of the spoon, and left enough trailing to leave a positive scent behind as we started to troll again.

We were going back over waters that we had been through before when, as if on cue, both Papa St.Onge and Papa Warburton had a strike.

They gave their rods a sharp pull to sink the hook, and then the rods bent nearly double. Good thing that both men were strapped in their seats, and the rods firmly fastened.

Normally at a strike of this kind, the other fellows would reel in quickly to clear the deck for the action to follow, but both were committed.

There could be no doubt that the fish were large. The reels just hummed a loud tune as the fish dived for lower depth, and then they slowly reeled them back to the surface.

It was a nightmare trying to keep the boat stable, and the lines from crossing as the fish tried to shake free of the hook. I increased the speed a bit hoping to tire the fish, and then slowly but surely they were brought closer and closer to the boat.

When the first one was close enough for Klaus to get the net around the fish, he took an iron rod and hit him hard just below the head to stop his flailing, and then tied him quickly while reaching for the gaff to get the other fish.

It was a struggle but Klaus managed to get him in the gill and hold him long enough to persuade him to be still.

We pulled them up onto the rack we had at the side of the boat, and tied them down, unfastened our spoons, and headed for home. None of us had ever been this close to fish that size, except in a fish market.

On the way home Dad said, "After we get him weighed, I'd like to get him to a taxidermist and have him mounted."

Papa St.Onge said, "I have already chosen the place where mine will be displayed in the Auberge. I can hear the Mayor tell us that fish like this should be displayed in the town offices for all the tourists to see."

"Why don't we invite him along on a fishing trip?"

Dad looked at me ands aid, "OK, next trip I drive and you fish."

We pulled up to the dock, unloaded the two large fish, and then watched as the dock master produced a handy collapsible tripod with a scale attachment.

The fish was weighed, checked by another fellow to ensure accuracy, and then photographs were taken. They then repeated the process for the second fish, Papa Warburton's.

By then the taxidermist had arrived, and he made off with the two fish while the dock master invited the four of us into his office. He said, "I've been here for seventeen years and have never seen anything like this catch in one boat in one day. May I offer you gentlemen my congratulations and a drink of this fine old brandy I've been saving for years. Gentlemen I propose a toast to the two conquering heroes of the 318 pound battle, and the 314 pound battles, won this day. Salute!"

We thanked him and took the boat back to its berth, tidied up and went home.

Klaus had called Mama St.Onge from the dockside so Papa St.Onge was given a heroes welcome as he entered the Auberge. They had called Patricia, and she and Mom had things well in hand at home.

I was given a few moments to wash up, and then we

toasted Dad for his mighty effort of the day. Then I was volunteered to do the honors in cleaning and preparing the fish for dinner.

While I was busy Dad came out and said, "That fish will fit nicely into the wall space above the fireplace. In fact, there is room for an even larger one, as soon as I catch him. We can give this one to the Mayor, and until then you will see this hundred-dollar bill nailed to the wall right here. I t will buy a very special bottle of brandy on that day."

"I'm sure you noted the GPS position where we caught the fish today. Let us start our next day there with the same bait system. We can surely take three men to fish and I will drive next time so we all get a fair chance at this fish challenge."

"I don't know where George is in this fishing game but we certainly better ask him and soon. He will have heard all about today by the time we have our dinner."

I went over that evening to see George and told him about the fishing venture, and asked him if he would like to participate in the fun and games. He laughed and said, that he had never caught anything larger than a sardine, but he loved to get out on the water. It was a wonderful opportunity to think about problems without interruptions. He would be ready, anytime, I went over to talk to Robert. He had never been fishing for anything, but would like to come along and watch to get the feel of it.

Patricia had been curious about the hundred-dollar bill nailed on the wall, so when I told her what it was for. On her next trip to Rennes, she went shopping for a couple of bottles of ancient and tasty brandy, and hid them away until they would be needed.

The fishing club went on for weeks, the men were certainly enjoying themselves, and I suspect the wives did a lot of visiting around enjoying life in the village.

Dad tuned in to the weather reports and then one Friday evening he said, "A new front is moving in overnight, overcast with rain showers tomorrow. Want to try our luck?"

"Sure, I'll call Klaus and Robert, and we can get an early start."

Quick check–rain gear, lunches, full fuel tanks and we were off. As soon as we got to the deep water, we put our spoons on and began trolling for some of the smaller stuff for bait. By the time we arrived at the GPS position, we reeled in and wrapped the spoons with the entrails then put the lines out and started trolling.

I wanted a cup of coffee from our picnic basket, so I asked Dad to take my line while I washed my hands. He sat down, strapped himself in and then the monster struck.

We got the other two lines in quickly and watched as the reel hummed and Dad kept the pressure on. Back and forth, flashing across our vision, the fish rose out of the water and disappeared again trying to shake loose from the hook.

It took nearly four hours to get him worn out and close enough to the side of the boat to get the net around him, and get the chain wrapped around his tail. We pulled him close enough for Klaus to give him a mighty blow behind the head.

After the long struggle, we washed our hands, set the heading for home and had lunch. I saw Klaus, with a twinkle in his eyes, lean over and say to Robert

"Papa St.Onge will certainly be chewing on his mustache this evening."

We pulled up to the dockside and it took no time at all before we had a crowd of admirers. The dock master appeared, saw us and said, "The conquering heroes again."

He produced the tripod hooked up the chain around the tail of the fish, and then hoisted it up to get the weight. 364 pound. He stepped aside to let his assistant check the accuracy, confirmed it, and it was entered in their record book. Photographs were taken, and once more we were invited into the dock master's office for congratulations and a drink of his old and tasty. I asked Klaus to call Patricia and tell her to expect us, and went back to tidy up the boat, and tie her up for the night.

Patricia gathered the four of us in the living room and then she and Mom produced six glasses. Patricia handed an old bottle of brandy to Dad saying, "You get one of these for a hundred dollars."

Mom raised her glass, obviously very proud of her husband and said, "A toast to the conquering hero."

Klaus and Robert had another drink and said, that they would walk home. They wondered who was going to break the news to Papa St.Onge.

Patricia volunteered me to clean and prepare the fish for dinner that night, so we had a real old fashioned dinner with all the trimmings the girls could dream up.

We invited the Mayor to the Fisherman's Ball. Dad's fish was on display and he presented the smaller one to the Mayor for the town hall.

Papa St.Onge never gave up his search for a bigger fish,

but we did have the most fabulous recreational club I ever heard of. The wives were delighted because they knew when the men went fishing their husband would come home with very fine fish, and they would do the cleaning and preparation of the fish for dinner. Not quite a night out but not bad. We always caught a respectable lot of smaller fish, delivered one each to the home of the club members, and gave the rest of the catch to the Auberge.

I wondered, one day as I was cleaning a fish for dinner, what would happen if we took a large bucket of frozen entrails from the Auberge fish and just dumped half of it overboard when we got to our favorite fishing place.

Mama St.Onge was surprised indeed when I appeared the morning after a fishing trip to help them with the cleaning. She was even more surprised when I put the bucket in a large plastic bag, sealed it, and put it in the freezer lock up.

We picked it up next morning on our way to the boat, unwrapped the plastic cover to let it thaw out, and went off to fish. By the time we got to our fishing waters, it was mostly unfrozen, so we stopped the boat and poured half of it over the side. It took about three minutes before there was a great splashing, fish fins everywhere and then as suddenly as it had started it was quiet.

"Suppose we start with one spoon going down first to see if we get any reaction. Papa St.Onge will you start?"

He was ready, and slowly lowered his baited hook, twenty feet, forty feet and then wham, a strike that nearly pulled him out of his seat. Fifteen minutes later he had a nice fish, about eighty pounds, on the rack.

Then Robert lowered his hook slowly. Again, twenty

feet, forty feet, one hundred feet, and then he had a slam of a strike. It was another nice play of a good size fish, but not a prize-winner. Taking turns this went on for about two hours and then the activity suddenly stopped.

We had a most respectable day's catch and decided to go home. Today we would leave two of the smaller ones at each of the members' homes and then we would all gather at the Auberge early in the morning to help Mama St. Onge and the girls with the cleaning. We would save all the entrails in the deep freeze.

One afternoon in mid August Dad and I had just finished cleaning after a fishing trip and we were sitting having a drink when we heard the doorbell ring and then the door opened and a voice called, "May I come in?"

Young Arthur jumped up shouting, "Aunty-Frandy, Aunty-Frandy" and ran to the door. Patricia and I followed him and in a moment there was a melee of three adults hugging each other with Arthur in the middle.

Mom had a look of surprise on her face as she said, "Its Francine Couperand. We saw you at the Met in New York last year".

Dad said, "Sure looked like the royal welcome to me."

"Yes. This is home, and I have two weeks of holiday s before rehearsals start in Berlin."

With Arthur in her lap, she sipped her wine and told Mom and Dad how she had first met us, and then how she had been "adopted" by the village, and that her father was buried in the churchyard here.

Patricia had come in and heard the last part of the conversation.

"The roses are fabulous up there now. Let's go to visit

the grave in the morning."

She and Mom had produced one of the Cordon Bleu specials with the fish, and we all feasted like kings and chatted over dessert and coffee until Arthur fell asleep in Francine's lap and was taken off to bed.

CHAPTER ELEVEN

We had finished our coffee and brandy, Arthur was tucked in for the night, and then Patricia looked at her watch and said, "Time to feed the baby. Jim, will you please warm up a bottle while I change her?"

"Baby?" Came a query from Francine.

"Of course, you don't know. Since you were last here, we have acquired a red haired Viking. Come along and have a look."

Mom and Dad helped with tidying up, and we settled in to watch a movie while the baby was feeding.

"Who gets to feed her?" Francine asked.

"There is seldom a shortage of volunteers," Patricia said, "but since you haven't had a turn, perhaps you might have the job this evening."

While Francine was focused on the baby, I asked her, "Of all the operatic roles you have sung which one do you consider was the best showcase for your talents and, if it is not the same, which one did you enjoy most of all?"

"That's easy, the answer to both is Tosca."

Then I turned to Patricia and asked her, "Of all the composers music and particular selections which one do you regard as your favorite?"

"It would be a toss up between Beethoven second piano concerto and Chopin nocturnes. A hard choice indeed."

Two days later Mom and Francine had shopping to do in Rennes, so Dad offered to drive them.

Klaus and I had an open day to go for quiet fishing. I asked him if he had ever had a close look at a composer's original music sheets?

Puzzled he said, "No."

"I had an idea about the possibility of decoration for a wall. I have brought with me music sheets. Let us lay two of these out, as they would appear as the composer had written them; one and two. Now have a look, and then close your eyes for a moment, and try to imagine these two sheets having been made large, say three quarters of the size of the wall that is behind the piano in our living room. If you think it can be done, I will try to get a photocopy of the original music score written by the composer for you to follow in the final product. I would assume an elegant wooden structure as a frame around the entire project would fill up the wall space."

"How many of these wall decorations would you want?"

"Two, I think in our house. Once we have established a

good working system there might be more. Come to think of it, there is a nice large vacant space on one wall of the church that is just begging for a first but smaller portrayal of the psalm that begins "The Lord is my shepherd, I shall not want."

"We can get very thin slabs of pure white marble that can be put together seamlessly in a light weight strong steel frame, and then glassed in like a stained glass window. We could put the letters or lines and music notes on this surface as we wanted."

"You may know that at the last corporation meeting, we agreed on a name for the church, "The Church of the Good Shepherd" and it might be helpful if a hand sign for the church were to be made this way and set in a stone plinth."

Our discussion was abruptly interrupted by a great fish, that nearly pulled, the thoughtful Klaus, out of the boat. It took nearly an hour to get the fellow up to the boat and on the rack.

"Sad," I said, to Klaus "but I don' think he will qualify in the Fisherman's Challenge."

"Sure will make good eating for us all."

A week later George, Papa St.Onge and I were out fishing. Things were quiet, and Papa St.Onge suggested that the fish were smarter than we were, as they knew it was time for a nap.

George said, "Should we be thinking seriously of what we might be able to do to help our most famous resident get a stable place of residence, here. I'm sure she can afford to live in any number of places more exotic than this village, but she seems very happy here whenever she has holiday time. Should we be thinking of a residence or a place where opera singers practice what they do?"

"I think you all know what a real winner it was to build that residence for my Mom and Dad. They were a bit uncertain about leaving their home in Canada, but they will now tell you that they wish they had done it years earlier."

"Does anyone know what opera singers need by way of facilities? Where would we build a place for her to live, and make it her permanent home? Is it possible that any of the wives have heard anything about this from her?"

"I can tell you that she loves children, and as soon as she is settled here on a holiday she wastes no time gathering wives and children around the pool, and they play as long as they can every day. The kids all call her "Aunty Frandy" and I think she is going to make a couple of them into Olympic class swimmers. Wouldn't that be nice for the village?"

George smiled and then said, "All of that would be nice but let us get back to the ideas for a residence. I think we are going to have to get her involved in the planing as none of us know what she needs for learning and training for the various roles she sings. The living part is easy– kitchen bedroom and so on, but only she can give us a clear outline of what she needs. Location is going to be a problem. Where will the space come from? She will want to be at the core of the village activity, not on the outlying area."

"We should get her involved as soon as we can, because none of us knows what the prime working life of that kind of a talent is. There will come a time when her voice begins to show the strain of that very hard usage, and she will want to cut down on the number of appearances each year."

"Before we get her involved in any discussion you gentlemen should all know that on the occasion of her first meeting with Mom and Dad Warburton, she and they were sitting around a table while Patricia and I were getting things ready for dinner and I overheard her tell Dad that "the village was her home and would always be." We can use that as a starting point for all our considerations. The second thought I have is, that the cost of building the residence can be underwritten by the corporation. It may take a bit of time, but that money will come back to us in many ways. She must see this as our gift to her."

Papa St.Onge said, "Any discussion? Any dissent? Then after a moment of silence he said, "OK. How do we get her involved, and how do we do it?"

There was a long silence as then Klaus said,

"It seems to me that the first initiatives should come from the women. Patricia and Lisa have worked with her in the swimming and entertainment activities. Let us see if we can get the first suggestion to come from them. and then we can pick up the ball."

Papa St.Onge smiled a broad smile and said, "If there is no further discussion, I would like to invite you over for a drink to toast Klaus and his stroke of genius."

It took a few days, but late one evening when everyone had gone to bed Patricia raised the matter of a house for Francine with me.

"The last thing we want is for her to feel in any way unwelcome here. I can understand that she will want privacy from time to time, but access to the children and life here is of utmost importance to her. By all means, if and when one else raises the issue, we will be doing everything we can to support the idea, but it must not emerge from us. Has anyone got a suggestion as to where her house should be located? Has anyone spoken to her about it?"

" Not that I know of."

"Has she ever spoken in any way of the time when her operatic career will come to an end? Most singers sooner or later start to lose their singing voices."

Next morning, when Patricia and I arrived downstairs to see about breakfast we found young Arthur and Aunty-Frandy sitting at the table eating strawberries.

"The pirates of Warburton Castle have struck again."

"I wanted to surprise Aunty-Frandy, so I woke her up, and we went out to the strawberry patch and found breakfast," said, Arthur.

"Aunty-Frandy, in all your travels around the world, you must have come across really memorable breakfasts. Which ones do you cook up when you are in your apartment in Paris?"

"There are two. In a restaurant on Mont St.Michel, they have a soufflé that is unique, and in Australia they have a steak and eggs combination that is a marvel. When I retire from singing, I would like to have a nice little stone house where I can go swimming every day, and where perhaps I can have students."

"Have you made any plans for your retirement?" I asked her.

"Oh I want to live here in St.Onge village. Dad is buried here, my friends are here so, this is home for me."

I looked at Patricia, and noted that she had picked up

the conversation and stored it away for future reference so Arthur and I went out to get strawberries for Gramma and Grampa who had come to join us.

We now had all the information we needed for the location of Francine's house. It would now be up to Giselle to find out what was needed in the interior. I'd wait a couple of days to let the women get their heads together on that. Meanwhile George, Klaus and I, would go out on a fishing trip to get it all in motion.

When I went over to the workshop to get Klaus cued in for tomorrow's fishing trip, I found him and Robert still laughing about a glass purchase they had stumbled across. They had gone to Rennes-sur-Mer to get materials and were spectators to an argument about glass that had been ordered but apparently a mistake had been made in the size. The contractor had wanted forty seven pieces of thick plate glass three feet by six feet, and they had received forty seven pieces three feet by two feet.

Robert took one look at them and interrupted the argument asking what they would take for the glass.

The merchant, surprised said, "They are no dam good, the factory will not take them back, and I'll never be able to sell them."

"I'll give you ten dollars each for the whole lot." The surprised merchant paused, saw he had painted himself into a corner and said, "It's a deal, Take them away."

They loaded the glass on the truck.

On their way home, Klaus said, "OK, Robert, what is on your mind?"

"We have been struggling with the matter of decent signs for around the village, and these are heaven sent.

Just imagine the elegant sign we can make for the church–
The Church of the Good Shepherd–on a white marble
background sandwiched between two pieces of this
unbreakable glass, mounted in a stone framework set on a
concrete base. The Auberge St.Onge and so on."

"Good for you for thinking of that. We can make them
all from the same size and pattern, and they will look very
nice indeed."

The ladies had brought Francine into a discussion of
what she would want in her retirement home when the time
came. She said that there were only a couple of things
really important. First, she loved to have a good long swim
every morning. It was the best exercise for her. She wanted
a large room for teaching the students she might get, and
also there should be a room for groups of students that
might branch off into a church choir. Basically, it would
serve to inject a love of good music into the community,
and early into the lives of the children. It would be a life
long gift for all.

George Charbonneau had a daughter who was one of
the outstanding swimmers in Francine's swimming club, as
they called it, and Francine had already earmarked her as
Olympic potential.

Since our pool was the only one in the village, and the
only one likely to ever be in the village because of space
limitations, it was obvious that the house for Francine had
to be built as an annex to our house. It would also have the
convenience of having Patricia readily available to help
with the musical training they would be making available.

The next time Francine came back to the village for a
bit of rest and holiday time from her hard work on the

opera circuit, George was determined to have Coupland House ready for her as a surprise and a thank you from the village. Every one wanted her to regard St.Onge as her home. We hoped it would be a pleasant surprise. The next time she parked her car beside our house, the first thing she would see would be the splendid new "Coupland House" sign.

Klaus and Robert finished the design for the wall of Francine's music room with the large portrayal of the first two pages of the original score of Tosca as the composer had written it. It turned out to be a masterpiece, very much like the smaller design they had made for Patricia of the Beethoven symphony. It would be interesting to see who came calling when the first pictures of Coupland House hit the fashion magazines.

I startled Patricia one evening, as she finished putting the children to bed, by asking her if she had ever thought of writing a concerto to describe her life in this setting after the years in Vancouver. She stopped where she was, looked as surprised as if I had struck her, and then said, "Child Harold in the New World".

It took six months of her time while the children were sleeping or at the pool with the swimming teachers. Then one evening I saw that all the papers around the piano had disappeared. The children were in bed, the kitchen was tidied up, and we were relaxed in the living room.

Patricia produced drinks and arranged four more chairs just before the doorbell rang, and in came Klaus, Lisa, George and Giselle. Patricia looked at me and said, "Surprise."

She then went over to the piano and spent the next

thirty minutes giving us the premier performance of her first piano concerto.

We celebrated our new discovery that night. Klaus was so enraptured throughout the performance that he had forgotten his drink, said, "There is a new bright star on the horizon tonight".

Two days later, Francine came back to finish her holiday before the fall opera rehearsals began. Lisa said, she would like to arrange a surprise for her Mom and Dad as well as Robert and Denise. I suggested that she invite the manager of the Rennes-sur-Mer Music Master shop and his wife. Once again, after Francine, Patricia and the family had dinner we got the children to bed and when the guests arrived we were given another performance of Patricia's piano concerto.

Once again the reception was enthusiastic, but I noticed that Francine seemed very quiet, almost puzzled and after a while she said, "There is a major section of descriptive sound not yet presented to the audience. Have you planned a successive concerto or a continuity of this one that will reveal a new part of your developement. It is the fulfillment and happiness of the children that is not yet spoken of in the music, is it not?"

Patricia laughed, and then went over to Francine and gave her a big hug and said, "I don't think twin sisters could understand each other as we do. The continuity, or the second concerto, or movement, whatever shape it is going to take, is already sketched and partially on paper–starting as you have indicated."

Francine said, "Klaus Morgenstern, the Director of the Berlin Philharmonic, who will conduct Das Rhinegold, is going to retire after the next season. He has always been most helpful to me. I'm sure he gets many manuscripts to read each year, more than he has time for, but if I ask him, he might study this score and make a comment or be helpful."

Then she went over to Patricia, put her arm around her shoulder, and for the first time I saw them this way, the tiny Chinese beautiful woman and the tall strapping, beautiful European woman, as astonishing pair of sisters as I had ever seen. Then Francine said, "What Patricia needs is time. If any of us can help with the routine household burdens, we must do so. Now she needs to have worry free days and time for this music. When she is finished, I will give the score to Dr. Morgenstern and ask him to read it and comment. I think he will be pleased to give the work its public premiere. It should be well received by the Berlin public."

She was right on all counts. Patricia was sheltered as much as possible from all housekeeping duties, and in two months had finished the work. Then Francine and the friend from the Music Master shop, and Patricia reviewed the entire work and presented it to the members of the St.Onge village Corporation.

Finally, a copy of the score was given to Dr. Morgenstern who studied it carefully, and then said that he would be delighted to present the work and the composer, in his Berlin winter concert series.

Klaus was right, a new star had been born.

CHAPTER TWELVE

Francine, Patricia and I had gone to Rennes-sur-Mer to do shopping and had gone to find lunch at what looked like a nice restaurant. We found imaginative seafood recipes and then, to our surprise Francine ordered apple juice.

The surprised waiter apologized. No apple juice available, apple cider, yes, "Would Madame have a glass of apple cider?"

"Yes, please."

"During the working days in Paris and elsewhere, for many years, I have started each day off with a large glass of apple juice and a good long, hard swim. For me this has been an unbeatable combination."

We looked at her and then I said, "The formula seems to have an astonishing magical quality."

It took me a few days to find a good supply of apple juice, and get it under a pyramid for processing, and then everyone in the place started the new program of having their juice and then the swim before breakfast. To my astonishment the first physical responses appeared in Mom and Dad.

Mom and I were standing in the kitchen for a moment after everyone else had gone to the pool and she said, almost blushing as she said, it, "I don't know what has come over him. It is wonderful. He hasn't been like this since we were first married."

She paused for a moment, as if remembering thing from long ago, and then went on, "You will have long forgotten it but when you were still in high school, and I had finished the cooking course with the Cordon Bleu School, I spoke to you about what I could only describe as a layer of awareness of life and living that the French seem to have that our English culture has never found.

It is a deeper awareness of one's real life, the world of things we can and should enjoy–I called it French Sauce. It seemed to me to not only be an upper layer of happiness, enjoyment and zest in the kitchen, but in all aspects of life.

Well that is what we seem to have found here, and something has turned your father into a new man–or to the old one I knew so many years ago. Life here is so full of quiet joy, love and affection that I wish we had found it twenty years ago. I don't know how to tell you how grateful we are to you and Patricia and these wonderful children. The enormous creativity in the whole village is amazing. It is as if one had poured a layer of French Sauce over our lives and the village."

She paused and then went on, "I haven't spoken to Patricia about any of these ideas or impressions, but I do notice that when she appears in the morning she just seems to sparkle. There is only one thing that makes a woman look this way. The house seems to radiate a very deep feeling of love and warmth, and it has deeply infected the children. One cannot help but notice the depth of the bond between Patricia and Francine. No two women could be more different in appearance, birth and background, and yet they could not possibly be more closely united in affection and in sisterhood than they are. I have never seen anything like it."

She paused and I let the moment pass. She could not have shown any more love and pleasure at being with the children than she did. They were swimming together every day, and when Francine was visiting they were a constant group. The children were still a bit young, but we were gently pushing them in the direction of learning a second language and learning to read. Both Grandma Warburton and Francine were teaching the children to enjoy learning. Patricia would take care of the mathematics in another year or so, and I had procured from the National Geographic Society the large wallpaper map of the world. I hoped the children wouldn't know they were learning until long after it had happened.

What Francine had been able to do with love and games to make astonishingly capable swimmers out of these two youngsters was little short of remarkable. It had rubbed off on the other children in the village, and there was an unspoken undercurrent of competition among them that was a delight to watch. They were all the best of friends, there was no jealousy or acrimony, they all understood that they were, one day in the future, going to be going with Aunty-Frandy to swimming competitions, and they were all going to be winners. In some strange unspoken way, she made them feel that they were all very special.

I interrupted my contemplation of the world I lived in and remembered it was Thursday. We didn't use any chlorine in the pool because it might do damage to the vocal cords of the swimmers, so it was essential that I do a double back-washing of the sand filters of the pool. This took about an hour, so I was up early and busy. We had a sign "DO NOT ENTER" that the children knew, and would respect if they were up and early at the pool.

I had put the sign on the door and the locked it before I started back-washing the filters before I noticed that out there in the pool, very quietly doing her twenty laps was Francine. I came to the edge of the pool and she came over, came out of the pool, and slipped out of her bathing suit and stood in front of me. She was a magnificent woman by any standards, but I knew that, and as we stood there, looking at each other, I slipped off my swimming trunks and took her hand and we walked over to one of the lounges that were on the patio.

This was the first time I had seen her this way in the bright light of the early morning sun, and again I was powerfully impressed with what a beautiful, magnificent woman she was. She had devoted so much of her life to me knowing that I was the husband of her best friend and for whom she was prepared to make sacrifices by acting as a surrogate mother for her friend. At the moment these value judgments were far from my mind–there were more immediate pressures to respond to–and we did.

It was only later, that I asked myself what it was that impelled this magnificent woman, who could have had her choice of many desirable husbands, to choose the path of self sacrifice, to help build a family that she would be a part of but would never be hers except by those stronger than steel bonds of love that linked us all together.

I knew that when she retired, as she must, for the career of an opera singer was seldom a long one, she would come to St.Onge to live. I was determined to give her my thanks in every way I could, but the line I could not cross was to acknowledge that the two children were hers. I could, and would do everything in my power to keep her and them together as a family group. She could participate fully in shaping their lives as they grew, and as the personalities developed. I wanted as much of her in their future as possible. I knew of no more beneficial influence that could be brought to bear in their lives.

She would have everything that money could buy to give her the finest residence that the corporation could give her. The rogue factor, of course, was me. She had everything she could want except that one thing that belonged to another–the man she loved.

The years were slipping by easy and graceful as they do in this latitude with no winter season to act as a sharp reminder of their passing. The only conspicuous markers were the developing children. Francine and Grandma Warburton had spent many, many hours training the swimmers. They were all very good, but the oldest

Charboneau girl, Cynthia and the Viking were the obvious future Olympic contenders.

One evening, while we were all at dinner the discussion had turned to the children and the swimming program, and I said, partly in jest, "Klaus and Robert will have to invent a sign for the village "Home of the Olympians".

In all seriousness Grandma said, "Get them started as soon as possible. Make sure they choose a nice location for the sign."

Francine smiled and said, "I have enquired in Paris at the Ministry to find out what the best finishing program would be, and they have advised me that as soon as they are fourteen they should spend the summer at a training school in Paris, and then at sixteen they should spend two full years at the school with the best instructors in the country who will get them ready for the Olympics. It may be a bit expensive, but it is the best training program known to the people at the Ministry." Then she paused for a moment, looked at us for a reaction, and then said, "I have already enrolled them." Another pause, and then she continued, "Because of the number of people who will be trying to get into the program, I have leased an apartment close by the school. There will be enough bedrooms for some of us to care of the girls. I will have to be away for part of the time, but we can spell each other so that the total task doesn't become too much of a burden for any one person."

This comment suddenly brought into sharp focus all the children we had in the corporation families. They seemed to be such an integral part of the landscape here in this small village, that I had not really focused clearly on all of them.

I quickly remembered the two Leitman boys, Klaus and Robert's sons, born within a few months of each other, and inseparable, like the two girls, Cynthia and the Viking. These two boys, when they were ten, had asked if they could learn to be outdoorsmen and spend time camping out among the redwood forest we had planted shortly after they had been born. They were fishermen par excellence, and I knew they were determined to break the record for the largest fish ever caught by a member of the Club. They were always standing by, in case there was room for them, when the boat went out.

I saw the two of them on the pier one day as we went out with a load of fishermen and no room for them. I saw the hurt in their eyes, so when we came back, I asked them if they would like to have a special trip out the next day with just the three of us, to see if one of them could break the record.

We wanted to get the early rise, so they were at the front door when I came out at 6 am. We drove down to the boat, and out to out secret deep-sea location. They had brought a pail full of entrails from Grandma St.Onge's lock up. They knew the routine, and were ready when we stopped the boat.

They looked surprised when I asked them if they had taken breakfast. I could see the answer was no, so I unwrapped the special package Patricia had wisely sent along. After all growing boys are always hungry

The first strike was massive, and took us most of an hour to get the thing on board.

"We will surely get the harbor master to weigh this

fellow in."

The next four hours were as hardworking as any I had ever seen. They caught fine large fish that Grandma St.Onge would be pleased to put into her cold storage. However, it was not yet the prizewinner each of them wanted. Well, we could go out again, and soon.

A few more hours and we were ready to back home. This load of fine, large fish, certainly would be a record for one day's catch, in the Fisherman's Club. We would be even more tired next day, when we had finished cleaning the fish for the cold storage lockers but we would deal with that problem tomorrow. Back at the dock, we managed to get a quick weigh-in for the big fish. He would be number three. There was still hope for the aspiring young fishermen.

As they were getting ready to go home after unloading the fish at the Auberge, I said, "We can meet here tomorrow about eight."

They looked surprised so I said, " You weren't thinking of leaving all the cleaning up of all these fish to Mama St.Onge, were you?"

"Never thought of it, really. We were going to do our regular forest patrol. We can do the cleaning and then still go."

"Good, you know your Grandma is a wonderful woman, and she needs all the help she can get, all the time. I will be there to help with the cleaning."

There was no argument or comment–I think they knew who controlled the boat.

CHAPTER THIRTEEN

Two evenings later, the four of us were sitting in the living room with our coffee, after the children had scooted off to bed, when the doorbell rang. Mama and Papa St. Onge came in. They took coffee and a drink, and then we were told the purpose of the visit.

The Auberge had been almost overwhelmed by tourists in the past two weeks, that was great as they were making a good deal of money, but their wine stocks were running very low, both red and white.

"I'm not sure about the inventory in the cave, but it is probably two or three hundred bottles of each and they are all ready for your use. We can give you about an equal amount of each from our cellar, most of it is two or more years in process so it should be first class for your clients."

Then Dad Warburton said, "We have about two hundred bottles of each in our basement, and seldom draw on the inventory as we are usually freeloading on these people here."

I asked Papa St. Onge, "Could your staff handle a two litre bottle as easily as they do a one liter bottle?"

He reflected for a moment and then said, "I don't know why I never thought of that before, but it would certainly be to our long term advantage to have all our inventory in two liter bottles. The vineyard labor costs would be reduced, our processing would not change, and our profits would increase."

"This seems to have been an exceptional year for grape production so the wines should be of good quality. Our problem is that we need more storage space and will need it quickly. Our best option is to double our space in the cave, and then invest heavily in this year's crop. If we have to carry some of it over into another year it will be a benefit for us."

"While your lads and the ladies are getting the wine together for delivery to the Auberge, we can get George and Klaus together to discuss expanding our cave space."

Next morning George and I carefully measured the interior of the cave, and then George went outside to calculate the cover weight. We had a maximum interior height of nine feet, we could cut out a six-foot length, and with careful shoring up of the interior walls we could triple our storage space.

George had a conveyor belt hook-up installed, and in a few minutes had a powerful electric drill in place, and it was in motion within two hours.

I was standing outside in the bright sunlight and was watching the fresh earth roll off of the conveyor belt onto the back of the truck for removal when I noticed something very unusual on the conveyor belt. It was a bright, reflected light flash.

Perhaps no one but a trained geologist would have caught this, and the earth would have disappeared into a landfill somewhere, but I was instantly alerted. I went with the truck driver back to the rear of the house, laid out two large tarpaulins for the earth to be dumped on, and then back to the cave and the next load.

Three hours later the digging was finished, the earth and all the machinery removed. Klaus and I set about putting the heavy timbers in place to support the new walls of the cave. We now had enough space for Klaus to do his magic with the pyramid storage cabinets to get the cave to do what it did so well.

Now time was of the essence, and I asked Patricia to get on the phone to the vineyards t we had used as suppliers in previous years, and find out when their first wines were going to be available for the market.

I then went down to Klaus' workshop to see if he had a small sieve screen I could borrow. I wanted a close look at the soil I had piled up in the back yard. I attached a garden hose to give me washing water for the soil as I sieved it. It took me nearly seven hours of hard work to get to the first of the specimens that had sent that reflective flash of light to my eye and my brain. It took me another ten minutes to find a second piece of the reflective material.

Every geologist knows about the "pipes" that volcanic

activity thrusts up in the formation of mountains and every geologist knows how these "pipes" produce diamonds, in many cases. There were none here, but lava does strange things, and one should be prepared to look carefully.

I had stopped believing in accidents or coincidences a very long time ago. These things were no more accidental than was the meeting of Oedipus with his father in the ancient Greek drama. It was no more accidental than my meeting with the indigent geologist that day on Bloor Street in Toronto. I had to be responsive, and quickly to whatever had driven me to this strange new discovery.

I now had three triangular pieces of this material, each side about an inch in length. Most people will know that if it is a garnet it will be worth about twenty-five dollars. If it is a ruby its value will be huge but the human eye cannot tell the difference. Only a spectroscope can tell the difference between a garnet and a ruby.

We were up early next morning, I asked Dad to take care of the kids while Patricia and I went to attend to an urgent matter in Rennes-sur-Mer.

The proprietor of the huge jewelry store seemed surprised to find us on his doorstep when he unlocked the door for the day's business, but invited us in and asked how he could help us.

"Do you have a spectroscope on the premises?"

"Of course."

"Could you give me a reading on this specimen?" I asked, handing him one of the three pieces I had in my pocket. He looked at it carefully, and then took out a loop, but he was studying me more than the piece I had handed him.

He called one of his assistants and then said, "Will you excuse me for a moment?" He was about to walk off to his back room spectroscope, so I said, "May I join you?"

He knew that I was no stranger to the process, paused and then said, "Of course."

He was boxed in, and we went to the spectroscope. He put the piece in the frame, and turned on the machine. Both he and I were surprised. He reset the dials, for the analysis to ensure that no mistake had been made, and the same final reading came out.

"I have been in this jewelry business for more than thirty years, and I have never seen anything like this before. If this piece is not unique for its clarity of crystalline structure it certainly is very rare, and very, very, valuable. May I ask about the origins of this piece?"

I ignored his question, and asked him if he had a good imaginative jeweler on his staff, who would know how to mount a piece like this on a fine gold base that would reflect the light up through the stone.

I asked him what the cost for service was. He shook his head and said, "No charge, let me know how I can be of further service to you."

He knew it was going to be a once in a lifetime experience, and profit to match.

We thanked him, told him we would be back and drove home. I cautioned Patricia to keep this discovery very, very quiet.

Mom and Dad were busy with the children in the pool when we arrived home. We left them playing, and went back to look at the earth that had come out of the cave to find all the ruby specimens that had been in this "pipe" that had been laid open for our discovery.

This was the second time in my lifetime that such an astonishing fortune had been laid open before me in this strange way.

For two days, Patricia and I worked our way through all of the earth that had been removed from the cave. We had eighty-nine pieces of ruby the likes of which had seldom, if ever, been seen. As a geologist I knew the spectroscope could not lie. We now had a very serious security problem.

As soon as there was any public knowledge of these rubies, they would be known as "The St.Onge Rubies", and it wouldn't take long before they were informally regarded as a national treasure. These rubies could be mounted by a good custom jeweler. We could have the work done off shore at lower cost, but that would be unwise in the long run.

Patricia and I discussed this at length, and agreed that we should assign the task to the jeweler in Rennes-Sur-Mer.

The jewels would become the property of the Corporation, and they should be used to adorn the ladies of St.Onge, who had worked so hard for so long to make the village the showpiece that it had become.

Patricia tried to escape into anonymity, but I laughed and said, "With school, the reflecting pool, the rose gardens around the village, the church windows and interior of the house to your credit, you want to be anonymous? I don't think so. You, Francine and Mama St.Onge will be at the top of the list. Mama St Onge's two daughters deserve huge credit, Denise no less, and I would not want to forget

Grandma Warburton. I suspect that if she had not had the good sense to deal properly with a fellow named Arthur Warburton, the village of St.Onge might be a very different place today."

She laughed, and then said, "What about the men?"

"Men don't wear rubies. They just adorn their wives with them. Can we find enough smaller stones to make seven respectable sets of earrings? Then having done that, can we find seven approximately similar size stones to give each of the seven a respectable ring? Having done that can we layout the remaining larger stones in a pattern for an elegant necklace for three of the women–Madame St.Onge, you, and Francine?"

We laid out the stones carefully, photographed them, and then paused to talk about security. We had no estimate of value, but if the first response from the jeweler was to be taken at face value, then we had pricey jewels indeed, probably worth millions.

"Who;" I asked Patricia, "in our corporate family do you consider would be the most trustworthy to share the decisions we are going to have to make?"

""Klaus and Lisa don't need or want what this would mean."

I called Klaus. He was surprised. but yes he and Lisa could come over. Five minutes later they were at the front door, and seemed surprised when I looked around behind them and then locked the door.

Patricia poured them a glass of wine, and then I told them the story of the strange discovery of the stones, and our trip to the jeweler. Then Patricia took the cloth off the tabletop, and they looked at the rubies for the first time.

I said, "It has not been possible to get an estimated value, but it will be many, many millions, and will almost certainly become a cause for contention. There will be a demand for them to be placed in one of the great museums of the nation. That kind of public reaction is uncertain and unpredictable.

We must, therefore, consider ourselves a committee of the Corporation, and be prepared to make a decision about them, or decisions about them that will keep them in our corporate possession, until a first public display has been made, and by inference, the possession is established in the hands of the Corporation."

" But you have possession and ownership of them."

"Ah, yes, my dear Klaus, but when you are dealing with this amount of value, governments have been known to do things that seem a bit unorthodox. They could be declared a national treasure because of their rarity, and we would be paid a very modest amount of money for them.

It will be impossible to keep this secret for any lengthy period of time. The best we can do is to break the entire task into small portions, each of which will not excite any attention. For example, suppose we decide to give each of the ladies who are members here, let's include Francine Coupland, a pair of ear-rings and a ring that is as similar as we can make it. The task of mounting will be given to various reputable jewelers in Rennes and in Marseilles. The instructions for mounting will be exactly the same in every case."

"Now while Klaus and I consider aspects of security for this lot of stones, can we persuade you two girls to select what you consider will be the best stones for earrings and a matching finger ring that will be given to each of the seven women involved–choose them for each person, as best you can, keeping in mind differences in size, especially between Patricia and Francine."

"What about the men?" Lisa asked

"Men don't wear rubies." Klaus said,.

Klaus and I went out to the workshop to consider the matter of security. I assure him that my "statement" about many millions was a gross understatement, if anything. But it was essential that the two of us should know where the stones were in case anything happened to the other one.

"Klaus," I said," it won't take long before bits of information leak out and, in time, I believe that this cluster of stones will become famous as the "St.Onge rubies". In time they will be declared a national treasure and the largest of the collection should go to a Museum where they will be safe. Meanwhile we will have dispersed enough value in the community for our own purposes. In the meantime, when we have finished the jewelry for the women, we should proceed to get the best jeweler we find to make–this will be for Francine in her public operatic performances,–a most magnificent ruby necklace that will gather a great deal of attention. Then we make two more magnificent necklaces, one for Patricia for her public performances, and one for the great lady who has made all of the St.Onge miracles possible–Mama St.Onge. The last act in the drama will be to have a great formal dinner at the annual Fisherman's Club, and we invite dignitaries and the press."

"The last time Francine was here she told us that she had done her first appearance as Turandotat the opening of the season in Paris, and that she had never before had such exciting reviews by the critics. She thought she would get two or three offers to do the role in other major operatic houses in the next year. We should have a spectacular necklace ready for her."

We went back to join the girls. They had finished their selection of stones for rings and earrings, wrapped them, and put tags on each with a name on it.

I outlined my thinking about the necklaces, starting with Francine, and we agreed to meet the next evening to consider the matter at length and draw up the design.

The next day, Klaus and I each with a wife beside him to help, took one package of ring and earring stones to a good custom jeweler, he in Rennes and I to Marseilles to get the whole thing in motion. I had prepared simple instructions to assure maximum reflectivity of the jewelry, and we would have to see who was prepared to give us a really good finished product at a reasonable price. We would let them look at the stones, examine our designs, and give us an estimate for the finished product.

As luck would have it Klaus and Lisa came to a large impressive company advertising custom work. They spoke to the manager, and to their surprise were told that his company was in the middle of a government sponsored apprenticeship program, and would welcome the job and there would be no labor costs, only materials, and all work done under strict supervision to meet professional standards.

They signed a contract, made a down payment and were asked to return in ten days. They were asked about the origin of the stones, and told the jeweler they had been given them by a relative, who was a ship's officer after he had come home from a trip to South America.

In ten days we had the finished product, superbly done. In three weeks we had the second set, also superbly finished, but at nearly double the cost. Obviously, we could not use the first source a second time, as they would suspect we were bringing illicit jewels from offshore sources.

The girls were modeling the finished jewelry, Klaus was admiring the finished product, and I wondered, out loud, if it wasn't time to have a bit of a holiday in Switzerland. Perhaps there was a major firm there with a subsidiary here in France. They would know this was not an illegal smuggling operation, and, having done the custom work could move the items back across the border to the client.

Three weeks later, we had a phone call from their Marseilles store that the personal jewelry was ready for pick up. They included a detailed description of the items, and an evaluation for insurance purposes. We were almost speechless so the manager told us he had received a covering letter from the main office pointing out that these gems were of an almost unknown quality in the gem trade. If there were any other known specimens, the firm would like to discuss the matter. Their price for service was so reasonable, that I kept looking for the fishhook.

Perhaps this was where the largest necklace, that would grace the person of Francine, should be done. The special earrings, and the finger ring to catch the eyes of the international crowds, as, from country to country, they watched her do her incomparable performance of Turandot.

Two days later, the four of us were in the Swiss Jewelry shop in Marseilles, and laid out the whole matter for him. It took him a few minutes to gather his wits about him and then he said, "I must place this matter in the hands of the head office. Can you possibly go to the head office in Switzerland? We will arrange a security detail, and make all customs clearances for you."

He gave his secretary instructions and in a few minutes she was back with confirmation of the airline tickets, and the request we be at the airport by ten am on Thursday morning.

What they could see clearly at that time, and we could not, was the value of the worldwide advertising that they would get. What I was interested in was the ambiguity about the source of the rubies. If we had a shipping invoice from a Swiss firm it might be difficult for the French Government to lay any claim on the gems.

CHAPTER FOURTEEN

At the Geneva airport, we were met by a large security group, the Vice-President, and then waved through customs and immigration, and driven downtown to the firm's head office.

Introductions made, and then we were invited to the President's private dining room for lunch. This too, was an almost royal affair. And then it was time for the star performer to enter the drama.

I unrolled the diagrams we had made, laid out the photographs, then took out the leather bag, and spread the rubies over the displays on the table.

The President shook his head, picked up three random rubies, handed them to his vice-president and said, "Please get the numbers off the spectroscope, have them checked to ensure no mistake has been made while we look at these diagrams."

Patricia and Lisa were wearing their earrings and the President asked if he might examine them. Out came his loupe and then he said, "Very nice work. I don't know how he could have improved the reflectivity."

The Vice-President came back with slips of paper, with the three specimens that he handed to the President, who looked carefully at each. He then turned to me and said, "You have seen these numbers?"

"Yes."

"All specimens come from the same source?"

"Yes."

"Your priorities?"

"You will know of Francine Couperand. She makes her home at the village of St.Onge, fifteen kilometers from Marseilles. She is already under contract to do fifteen performances as Turandot next year, London, Paris, Berlin and Sydney Australia. Negotiations are underway with the Metropolitan in New York. We would like her to have appropriate jewelry. The second priority would be a necklace for a smaller woman, Dr. Patricia Quinn, who on many occasion, accompanies Miss Couperand. She also lives in St.Onge village."

The President looked at me and said, "Dr. Patricia Quinn, the composer of the exquisite three French symphonies?"

Patricia gave him a large smile and said, "Thank You."

He recovered quickly, bowed over her hand, and said, "Shame on me for not recognizing you instantly.'"

Then he turned to his secretary and said, "My wife is in the Kaufhof two doors away, she would divorce me if she knew Dr. Quinn was here and I hadn't called her. Would you call, and see if they would page her?"

We set about fitting the various larger pieces into the diagrams we had laid out, and fifteen minutes later the door opened and in she came. Introductions were made and then she took Patricia's hand and said, "How long are you going to be in Geneva?"

"Three or four days, we thought."

Then to her husband, "Peter, I will arrange dinner for a few friends at the Chatillion tomorrow evening.... They will love to meet you. The Philharmonic gave more than half of an evening to your work a week ago."

I said, to her, "The missing person in the entourage is Fraancine Couperand. Next time we come we will bring her with us. She would love to meet you."

She looked at me to make sure I wasn't jesting, and then said, "We will make that an evening to remember. Imagine Quinn and Couperand in the same room."

Then she put an arm around Lisa and Patricia and said, "May I borrow the ladies to have tea while you men do all the slave labor?"

Out they went to the president's suite to talk over tea.

We had put the earring packages for the other St.Onge ladies aside, Mom Warburton, Mama St.Onge, Giselle and Denise.

Their design chief made a few suggestions as to changes of particular pieces and said, "The larger pieces are not dedicated?"

When I looked puzzled he said, " It would not be difficult to make a fine piece of jewelry for a lady's watch. For example, this piece, about the size of a Canadian fifty-cent piece, could be cut in two slices to give two faces of the watch. Diamonds could be placed showing the hour markers, then a gold or iridium case and voila.

I looked at the president and said, "Your wife is a very beautiful woman, and, unless I am mistaken she is the person who would appreciate having a few nice things. Could you include her in the earring, watches and finger ring? Would she like the surprise? We can arrange for Patricia and Francine to do the presentation, if you would like us to do so."

"She would never forget that day."

"There is one thing that I don't know anything about, but Francine could drive it forward, if it would help. It is the advertising your firm might get in the various capitals of the world in the programs that are given out at the performances. If you could make a suggestion or two, not many impresarios argue with her. Let me know how I can help"

As soon as our brief holiday was over, we were escorted to the airport. At home, I selected a package for the President's wife, and had it couriered through to Geneva.

Just before Christmas, we were invited to pick up the sets for the ladies of St.Onge. Two weeks later, the second shipment, the jewelry for Francine's first engagement as Turandot at Covent Garden in London, arrived.

We had the seven ladies and their husbands over for dinner, and the first showing of the St.Onge rubies in one room. The ladies were all attractive, and the way the lights reflected off of the stones is impossible to describe.

There were still two more necklaces to come, one for Patricia and for Mama St.Onge.

The performances of Turandot at the Covent Garden in London brought rave reports by the critics. We decided to ask Mama and Papa St.Onge, and the President and his wife to join us for the first performance in Paris. Francine joined us for dinner. The bonding between the women was almost instantaneous. By the time the dinner was over, one would have thought they were life long friends.

They would be happy to come and visit St.Onge village they said. Little did they know how their lives would be interwoven with those of the people of St.Onge.

I asked Francine if she was going to have a small rest period between the Paris and Berlin performances.

"It will be almost four weeks, and I will be so very glad to get home for a rest."

"Patricia and I have business to attend to in Geneva. If you haven't yet been to Geneva would you like to join us for a few days there?"

"I'd love to go and see the old city."

I saw the President looking at me, so I nodded and then a moment later he took out a notebook, checked a date. I knew he would have all the arrangements in hand. His wife had been the President of the Philharmonic Board of Directors for nearly ten years, and they wanted to say thank you. We should say thank you as well.

We made our way back to St.Onge and then, suddenly, everything changed. The Viking and Cynthia quickly departed for Paris and the final training for the Olympics that were now looming large on the horizon.

Two years ago, to our astonishment, Arthur, who had been happily working his way through all the training that George Charboneau could give him in his office, decided that he wanted to go to Paris and take lessons in sculpturing.

It seemed almost as if the young birds had taken their first flight out of the nest and were gone. It was quiet and we missed them very much, but we knew they had to make a life of their own.

We knew, of course, that the Viking and Cynthia were going to go to the Medical School at the Sorbonne, and begin their studies in medicine when the fall semester opened.

I was never quite sure why I did it, but I called our Swiss jeweler friend, Peter Ogilthorpe, and invited him and his wife, Arabella, to come and spend a long weekend with us that September. Their two daughters were away at university. They would be delighted.

Klaus, Robert and I had everything ready to take Peter out on his first fishing trip. He loved fishing but the waters around Geneva were not prime fishing territory and his last catch had been a few salmon in Scotland many years ago. We all had much to be grateful to Peter for, so we hoped we could make his day.

I checked the GPS position carefully, Klaus and Robert did all the nasty magical wrapping of the fish guts on the silver spoon bait we were using, and then we shut the engines, and put out the weighted spoons.

Robert had the first strike, about sixty pounds so we brought him in with Peter watching, wide eyed with wonder. I checked his seat belt, and the clamp of his rod and then Klaus had a strike. We brought him in, about forty pounds, great for the Auberge, and then Peter had a strike. He had been watching how we pulled the smaller fish up, and tied them into the rack on the side of the boat, so he was caught unprepared when his line suddenly bent almost in half, and he was in for a fight. Klaus and Robert reeled in their lines and stood by.

This was a new experience for Peter, but he was clever and kept the pressure on until we had the fish on side in the net, about an hour later. I guessed about fifty kilos, not one to enter the record books, but worthy of a photograph on the dockside to give bragging rights back home.

Klaus and Robert took the fish right to the Auberge, and in a few minutes Patricia answered the phone. It was a summons, for us and for our guests to a special dinner at the Auberge, to welcome them to the village.

Mama St.Onge knew Peter had been the driving force behind the rubies they had all been given, so she was determined to give them both the royal treatment at the Auberge.

Halfway through dinner she announced that the fish we were eating had been caught that afternoon by our guest of honor. We toasted Peter, and Papa St. Onge announced Peter's membership in the Fisherman's Club. They were being adopted into the St.Onge family, and it was a new and happy experience for them.

Arabella took Peter on an exploratory trip of the village, and they returned with many questions, and an offer to take us to lunch at the Auberge. They were delighted with the village, and seemed disappointed to hear that there were no properties nearby that they might purchase against Peter's retirement that was only five years away. We asked them when they could come back again, bring their daughters and stay longer. To our astonishment we were told that the younger of the two was not going to be home again until the end of the spring semester at the University of Berlin, but that the oldest, Priscilla now twenty three years of age, would defend he doctoral thesis at the University in Geneva in February.

She would need a change from her studies and could they bring her along for a visit to the village?

"The young birds have flown out of our nest," Patricia said, so you would be more welcomed than you know. The Viking is studying medicine at the Sorbonne and Arthur is discovering his talent at a special school for sculpturing at Caen. We are not sure when he will be back. He seems, if we can trust the letters we get, to really have found the thing he likes to do."

They reluctantly left the village a few days later, and promised to come back in the spring.

The days and weeks rolled around and life in the village came back to normal, a rather low key normal, with the children away at their studies. It was amusing to see the pressure grow between Papa St. Onge and Grandpa Warburton. Each was determined to capture the title before the next Fisherman's Club dinner. The ladies loved the competition as it brought a plentiful supply of fresh fish to each house in the village

The end of February brought a phone call from Arabells Ogilthorpe. Priscilla had completed all the requirements for her Ph.D., and they were all in need of a change of scene and a few days holiday. Could they come to visit?

We met them at the airport, Peter was obviously ready for fishing, and we were surprised at our first meeting with

Priscilla, a very pretty young lady. She looked eighteen, and in a very short time she and Patricia had become fast friends. We put their luggage in their rooms, gave everyone a few moments to look around, and then made our way to a rousing welcome at the Auberge.

Priscilla was wide-eyed at the way they were treated, "Its like being royalty," she whispered to her mother.

"No, no, its just that we have been adopted into the family."

Next morning after a long sleep-in for most of us, the ladies were sitting in the rose garden having a late cup of coffee when Arthur drove up and brought his luggage out of his car and came into the front door. He went back to the car and brought out a heavy box that he brought into the living room and carefully set on the table.

None of the ladies had moved from their seats as they were all looking in astonishment at Priscilla. She was looking at Arthur as if she was having a vision, with a radiant smile on her face saying in a soft voice, "Its him, its him, it's the man I'm going to marry."

Then she stood up, put her coffee cup on the table, and walked over to Arthur, smiled at him and said, "I'm Priscilla Ogilthorpe, and I've been waiting for you for a long time. Will you marry me?"

Arthur looked at her for a long moment and then smiled and said, "Yes, I think we should get married."

By now Patricia, Arabella and Francine had found their feet and their tongues and were crowding around the pair.

"Arthur, have you come home to stay?"

"Yes, Mother, could you call the Mayor to see if he will

marry us tomorrow? Then we can get the train to Greece for a couple of weeks. We can always do the church thing later on. I need an engagement ring for this girl Where are the men? Can you call Mama St.Onge and arrange a dinner party this evening?"

Francine said, "Just a moment." and went out of the room to her house next door. She was back in a very short time with a small box, gave Arthur a kiss on the cheek, and said, , "God Bless you both."

Arthur opened the box and took out what looked like a three-carat diamond ring. His eyes grew wide as he looked at Francine, gave her a big hug and a kiss on the cheek and turned to Priscilla, who had just been standing there through all the commotion never taking her eyes off of Arthur.

At that moment the front door opened and in came the three fishermen, Peter, Grandfather Warburton, and Jim. They saw the women all grouped around Arthur and Priscilla. Peter said, "What is wrong? What has happened?"

After a moment of silence Arabella said, "Priscilla is going to get married tomorrow."

"Tomorrow? Why haven't I heard of this?"

"No one heard of it until a few moments ago."

"Will someone please tell me what is going on?"

"Father," Priscilla said, "for the past year I have had many vivid dreams about a fellow I was going to marry. He was a sculptor who I had never met or seen but he was as real as he could be. Then a while ago a fellow came into the house with a heavy box, and when he turned around I saw it was the man in my dreams," she pointed at Arthur, "so I went over to him, and asked him to marry me, and he said, yes. So we are going to get married tomorrow, and go to Greece for a couple of weeks."

Peter took Priscilla's hand, looked at the engagement ring, then at Arthur and said, "You just happened to have this in your pocket?"

Francine stepped over to Peter and said, "Fifteen years ago I was given this ring, and two days before we were to be married my fiancé was killed in an auto accident. I just gave it to Arthur with my best wishes."

Peter looked at Arthur and said, "I apologize, but this comes as somewhat of a surprise to me."

Arthur smiled, said, "Me too." and they shook hands.

Then Patricia, ever the practical one said, "May I suggest that all fishermen's wives take their men to the shower so my living room will smell less like a fishing boat."

They all trooped off leaving Francine, Priscilla and Arthur, and then Francine looked at the box Arthur had brought in when he first arrived and said, "May I ask what you have here?"

Priscilla was standing beside Arthur and said, "May I read out what the sign on the box says?
First Prize
French National School of Sculpture
Awarded to
ARTUR JAMES WARBURTON.

Francine and Priscilla gently lifted the cover off, to reveal an astonishingly detailed sculpture of a section of the Village of St. Onge'; from the redwood trees in the background to the church, the pool, the Auberge and other features. The delicate detail was breathtaking.

Francine looked at it with tears in her eyes, and said, "It is simply stunning in it's beauty."

Arthur came over to her, gave her a big hug, kissed her on both cheeks and said, "I'm pleased you like it. The School gave me this first forging, and since you have been such a wonderful inspiration all the years of my life, I immediately ordered a second one for you."

Francine wiped away the happy tears as the others came back from their showers. They came over to see what the object was. They were all astounded, and then, Priscilla read the notation on the box for them.

Everyone gathered around to congratulate Arthur on his magnificent work. Peter asked Arthur how many copies of the work had been made.

"This is the only one but I have ordered a second one for Aunty-Frandy, and I would be happy to order a third one for you if you wish."

"Oh, yes I do wish. I will have a huge battle with Arabella as to whether it should be, in our house or on display for the public to see in the head office."

"It will certainly come home when you retire."

"Arthur", I said, "I imagine you do not want too many copies scattered around the world, but you are going to get a lot of pressure from Mama and Papa St.Onge."

He took a sip of his drink and said, "I know. I have sketches for lesser works of the village, and the St.Onge people will be first on that list, as I do not want more than three signed copies of this one. Priscilla and I will look at places in Greece in the next two weeks and then, if there are any strawberries left, I will go to work on something from Greece. I would like to do Priscilla as one of the figures from the Temple of Nike."

Then he turned to Francine and said, "Aunty-Frandy, I would especially want you to know that when I was at school these many months, it was difficult and often I needed the inspiration that you and Mom and Dad had taught me over the years in the swimming pool and the classroom. My debt to the three of you is a heavy one, and I want you to know it. He paused and then said, "Now can I kiss the bride to be?"

We all laughed and turned our backs on them, and Patricia said, "Let us know when you are finished."

"Call me in the morning."

We turned and toasted the couple. It was time to go to the Auberge for the pre-nuptial celebrations. They would get married by the Mayor at our house mid morning, and then after a luncheon, catch the train to Athens to begin their new life together.

The drive back to St.Onge was a quiet one for all of us, and when we arrived we discovered that Patricia had pulled out of the darkest corner of the basement a bottle of the hundred year old Calvados that had been aging for a long time, awaiting a very special occasion. We decided that occasions would never get more special than this one so Peter and I cleaned up the dust of many years and then poured generous drinks for the seven of us.

I lifted my glass and said, "Peter and Arabella, this was as much of a surprise to us as it was to you, to have the young birds fly out of the nest this way, but it seems to have been designed in Heaven, and laid out for us almost like an ancient Greek drama. Our houses have already been greatly blessed by the presence of these two, may we continue to share in those blessings for all the years to come."

We all drank to that happily and then Arabella asked, "Has there been any indication as to where they want to live and work?"

"I hope they choose St.Onge but the lure of Paris may be too great, but we have not heard a word from either of them." Patricia replied.

CHAPTER FIFTEEN

The newly-weds arrived home sun tanned and very excited about all the sculptures they had seen in Greece. It seemed they bought every book of pictures of Greek sculptures they could find, and that Arthur had taken hundreds of pictures as they went along from place to place.

George and I had spent a bit of time trying to get an idea of what kind of workshop space, and how much did a sculptor need, while they were gone, but we did not know enough to make any kind of decision.

One of the aspects of the working facilities was brought home to us rather sharply when two days after their return, Patricia and I received a letter from the Minister of Culture, an impressive heavily embossed letterhead and signed by the Minister himself.

He had been advised by the Director General of the

National School of Sculpture, that the first prize had been awarded to our son, Arthur Warburton. The Director, who had been at the School for nearly forty years, and was a respected scholar in the field, had suggested that he had not seen a work come out of the School, or for that matter, out of Europe, that could be compared in the genius of its design and execution. He strongly suggested that the Ministry should enter into discussions with the sculptor to ensure that such a work of art be acquired by the National authority.

Priscilla and Arthur had gone shopping in Rennes-sur-Mer so I asked Grandma and Grandpa Warburton to join Patricia and I for lunch so we might read the letter to them, and ask for any comments they might have. Aunts Frandy was in the pool with her swimming class, so we asked her to join us as well.

When the letter was read, and translated for the senior Warburtons everyone just looked at everyone else as if there was a kind of a dream floating around the room. His first sculpture and there was this kind of reaction?

Granddad said, "Klaus has made an elegant structure for holding this first copy, but perhaps we should take another look at the security element involved."

No one had anything much to say, and we agreed we would wait until after dinner that evening to show the letter to Priscilla and Arthur. He had told us that he had other sketches of the St.Onge Village, but we knew nothing of the detail.

Grandma Warburton, Patricia and Aunty-Frandy got their heads together to plan a celebratory dinner for that evening, a formidable array of talent. Dad and I went for a walk down to the docks to see what kind of fish might be found.

When Arthur and Priscilla arrived they joined us in the rose garden for a drink, and then we trooped into dinner. Arthur took one look at the candles and said, "Expecting royalty?"

Patricia smiled and said, "Yes, and you are it."

No one was quite sure how the letter from the Minister of Culture was going to be received by Arthur. It was obviously going to place a heavy burden on his future work schedule, so when we were finished I said, "Arthur, your mother and I received a letter in the morning mail from the Minister of Culture, and I would like you and Priscilla to read the letter."

He read the letter, and then gave it to Priscilla. She then looked at him, and said not a word. The decision would be his.

Then Arthur said, "It is an unparalleled opportunity not likely to be repeated. We must take advantage of it. It will take most of three years to complete the panorama. Can we find space for a workshop? "

"George and Klaus are ready to get to work as soon as you define what your shop needs are."

"If I had about one half of the garage space it would be large enough. But first we should clear up a couple of things. Priscilla and I discussed this at s length, and we both want to live here in St.Onge, if you will have us. We want to swim each day, and Priscilla wants to fit into the St.Onge family. Second, Priscilla and I should go to Paris while the workshop is being fitted out with windows, as I need lots of daylight for working. Paris has the only foundry in France capable of properly producing the forgings like the one we have here. They have more work than they can handle, so we must establish our credit and reputation with them. The minister's letter will help a good deal."

Five days later Priscilla and Arthur presented themselves at the foundry manager's office. He looked at them carefully, then read the letter from the Minister and smiled and said, "Mr. Warburton, may I offer my congratulations. May I say that your work was one of the most delicate and difficult forgings we have ever handled. It was a great challenge for our most experienced men, and they are the best in the world. When the finished product goes into the National Gallery, we would like to have our name mentioned."

"You may be sure I will do my best."

"Do you have any sketches of the final product that you envision?"

"Yes."

He looked at them carefully and then said, "How exquisite in the detail. How did you ever dream up a vision of a village like this in France? It would be marvelous if we really had villages like this."

Priscilla and Arthur looked at him and then said, "We live in this village."

It seemed from the expression on his face, that he thought he was having his leg pulled, so Arthur said, "When you have a weekend, please bring your wife and come to visit us. A quick flight to Marseilles and we will pick you up at the airport, and make you most welcome. Here is a phone number to let us know your arrival time."

It took two months for him to decide to make the phone call, a bit hesitant at first, but Priscilla took charge and then they arrived mid Friday morning. Mama St.Onge had the royal suite ready for them, and produced a fabulous lunch with half the village folk there to join them, to welcome them to the village, and then to show them around.

By mid afternoon they all ended up at Warburton House for a pool party.

The look of surprise, on Madame Boisvert's face when she saw Francine come in to join the party, was amusing, and even more so when Francine went over to them, shook their hands and welcomed them to the village.

"Yes," she assured them, "I live right next door, and am a member of the St.Onge family. I have been the village children's swimming teacher for years. St.Onge had two gold medalists in the recent summer Olympics. Is there anyone here you have not met?" She took them off to get a glass of wine and a dip in the pool.

All the village folk knew that pool parties were over at five o'clock as life went on no matter how much fun we were having. We got dressed, and then went to relax in the living room. Our guests now had an opportunity to see the house. Mr. Boisvert was captivated, by the large wall map of the world Klaus and Robert had made. He asked Patricia about it and she said, "Our friend Klaus does things like that. You will meet him later on."

Patricia and Mrs. Boisvert joined the men over drinks before dinner, while Grandma Warburton, Francine and Priscilla prepared dinner. The ladies had pulled out all the stops to impress the guests, and they did. Later, we sat in the living room over coffee and brandy until it was time to clear away the cups and saucers before the guests arrived.

Patricia played one of her French symphonies, and then we paused long enough to serve drinks for any one who wanted one before Francine, with Patricia at the piano began with the aria from Samson and Dalilah, 'My Heart at Thy Sweet Voice'.

There was a long moment of silence when she finished, and then a huge outburst of applause and everyone saying, "Encore! Please!" until, she sang it once more. Then she smiled at her audience and began the Casta Diva from Norma, and other favorites.

Then the two stood up, took their glasses, and joined the rest of us. Patricia, ever the clever hostess, took Mr.Boisvert over to Klaus and said, "This is the genius who made the map you were admiring."

"It is magnificent. Are such things available? Can you tell me about it?"

"We do make them. It is made entirely of different kinds of wood obtained from various parts of the world. We currently have requests that will take about ten years to complete."

Mr.Boisvert said, "Ten years?"

"Yes, but we always reserve the right to allocate our own priorities. Are you not the manager of the foundry that did the Warburton casting?"

"Yes."

"Then your family will go to the top of the list. Do you have a card with address so I can have a man come up and look at the wall, take measurements and so on next week? You do not have a drink, so let us go and celebrate the deal with a glass of Jim's splendid old Calvados."

My early morning cleaning of the pool filters was interrupted by a phone call. The Viking and Cynthia had caught an overnight bus from Paris to Rennes-sur-Mer and would like to come home for breakfast. They were on a three-week break between semesters. Was Aunty-Frandy home, as they needed a good Australian breakfast, to start their holiday?

The roads were almost empty of traffic at that early hour so we could move along quickly. The Viking said, "What I want most of all is a good swim before breakfast."

"Me, too, but I don't have a swim suit available."

I said, "At this early hour you will be the only ones in the pool. Enjoy yourselves while I get the breakfast steaks ready."

Ten minutes later I was surprised to see Priscilla come into the kitchen and tell me, "There are two naked young ladies I've never seen before swimming in the pool."

I looked at her and the whispered, "Go into the room, take off your swim suit and join them–it's the Viking and Cynthia".

Apparently Francine, unaware of what was happening in the pool, came in a few minutes later, saw the three of them, started laughing, took off her swimsuit and joined them.

Fifteen minutes later Patricia appeared, had her first sip of orange juice, and I asked her to find dressing gowns for Cynthia and the Viking, so they could come in and we could all have breakfast.

I noticed the Viking looking at Priscilla, and then she said, to her, "I noticed you keeping up stroke for stroke and lap for lap with Cynthia and I, Where did you learn to swim like that?"

"I lived in the dorm in Geneva, and we had a pool in the building. I had only to roll out of bed, and go across the building to have a morning swim."

"What were you studying?"

"Economics."

Both Cynthia and the Viking looked at her with expressions of horror on their faces. Then the Viking said, "We have been looking at the simple nuts and bolts of the human being in medicine. We were obliged to take one course in Economics and were completely overwhelmed by it, and you did a doctorate. By the way where is the Wunderkind?"

"He is in the workshop by six each morning, and comes out at eight for a swim and breakfast, and then back to work again."

She looked at her watch and at that moment Arthur came in the door "Speak of the devil and he is sure to appear. Excuse me if I go and do my wifely duty, and save him from starvation and extinction."

Two mornings later, Grandma Warburton and I, being the usual early first ones up and having a early snack of strawberries, were surprised to have Francine arrive join us in the kitchen. She had two weeks before the next series of rehearsals and needed a holiday.

Grandma Warburton said, "If we were in Canada this would be the Thanksgiving holiday week-end, and I would be roasting a large turkey."

"Thanksgiving?"

"The early American pioneers had this as a special celebration after the harvest, and it has become a tradition and a holiday."

"The Ogilthorpes are coming for a long week-end, and we will have a house full of happy people. God knows we have much to be thankful for, so why do we not have our own Thanksgiving week-end party."

At that moment, Patricia appeared, listened to the idea and said, "Of course, how clever of you to come up with the idea, shame on me for not thinking of it sooner. Jim you will have to hurry to get to the airport to get the Ogilthorpe's. Mom would you please come with me to Rennes-sur-Mer. We can make up our shopping list as we go. Francine needs to get a few hours sleep. Grandpa Warburton and some of the men have gone fishing."

The rush to get everything put together was interesting to watch, but the really impressive part, of the whole week-end, was the arrangement of music and songs that Francine and Patricia put together. Francine, singing Ave Maria electrified the audience. I was watching Priscilla during the performance, and then it came to me in a curious flash. She knew the music very well and knew how to play an instrument.

When the song was finished I leaned over to Arabella Ogilthorpe and asked her, "What instrument does Priscilla play?"

"The harp. Oops–I wasn't supposed to tell you."

"Why not?"

"They are very expensive instruments, and she did not want to be a burden. She played the harp in the Geneva Philharmonic."

"Would you come with me to the Music Master shop to select one for her? We might be sensible, and get one for her to play in the church from time to time as well."

The day the harp was due to be delivered the ladies went to Marseilles to shop, and when they returned home and Priscilla went into the living room we were waiting for her.

The expression on her face when she saw the magnificent golden instrument was a moment all of us would remember for the rest of our lives.

She put the box she was carrying on the floor, looked again at the harp, and then went over to the instrument and sat down and played the Schubert's Ave Maria while we listened spellbound.

I could not imagine a more worthwhile investment.

Tomorrow will be my 47th birthday. Patricia has arranged a pool party in the afternoon, and a dinner party at the Auberge in the evening, a celebration for all the villagers.

I'm sitting on the patio staring out, reflecting on how a small kindness has had such a large consequence. What would my life have been like if I have not offered a small kindness to that shabby old fellow in the pub on Bloor Street the week before graduation from University, and he had not given me the map which took me to the goldmine?

What chance was it that brought Patricia to the university and the meeting in the classroom, and then beyond?

What strange chance was it that brought about our meeting with the young student in Renne-sur-Mer and made possible the chance of a scholarship for her in Paris?

I can easily recall the sad state of the village on the day I first saw it, but I cannot recall what it was that prompted me to think I could make a life here.

The blend of love, kindness and beauty in the village has indeed created an overlay of joy, a life that Mother Warburton so often described as 'French Sauce'.